"They paid you well for this, didn't they?"

There was a world of bitterness in Luke's voice as he thrust the newspaper at Kate. "Singer in holiday romance," the headline screamed, "Midnight assignations on Pevensey Beach"....

"You're all the same, aren't you?" he remarked. "Just another cheap gold digger out for what she can get. And I called you honest."

"If you think I wrote this, then you're mistaken."

"Am I? Who else could have?"

"I wouldn't know. But I didn't write it."

"Liar," he said. "You should've waited, Kate. In another week or two you could have got an even better story!" And before she could answer he had slammed out of the room.

"Luke!" Her voice was a small despairing wail, but she spoke to an empty house.

WELCOME
TO THE WONDERFUL WORLD
OF *Harlequin Romances*

Interesting, informative and entertaining,
each Harlequin Romance portrays an appealing
and original love story. With a varied array
of settings, we may lure you on an African safari,
to a quaint Welsh village, or an exotic Riviera
location—anywhere and everywhere that adventurous
men and women fall in love.

As publishers of Harlequin Romances, we're
extremely proud of our books. Since 1949,
Harlequin Enterprises has built its publishing
reputation on the solid base of quality and
originality. Our stories are the most popular
paperback romances sold in North America; every
month, six new titles are released and sold at
nearly every book-selling store in Canada and the
United States.

A free catalog listing all Harlequin Romances
can be yours by writing to the

HARLEQUIN READER SERVICE,
(In the U.S.) P.O. Box 52040, Phoenix, AZ 85072-2040
(In Canada) Stratford, Ontario, N5A 6W2

We sincerely hope you enjoy reading
this Harlequin Romance.

Yours truly,

THE PUBLISHERS
Harlequin Romances

Kate's Way

Sara Francis

Harlequin Books

TORONTO • NEW YORK • LONDON
AMSTERDAM • PARIS • SYDNEY • HAMBURG
STOCKHOLM • ATHENS • TOKYO • MILAN

Original hardcover edition published in 1983
by Mills & Boon Limited

ISBN 0-373-02624-2

Harlequin Romance first edition June 1984

For
JULIE and JANE and KENDRA
who helped

CHAPTER ONE

THE grinding, keening crunch of metal fracturing metal, the sudden, near-explosive sound of her offside window shattering behind her seat brought a scream of fear to Kate's lips, but she had no time to let it escape as the high grass bank on her right loomed up in front of her startled eyes.

A few seconds before, she had been driving her Mini happily and reasonably at thirty-five miles an hour along the narrow country road. At the same moment as she had seen the large bonnet of the white car loom from the side lane on her right, she had realised that it was not going to stop. Instinctively she had pushed her accelerator pedal to the floor, hoping to get clear, and the small car had responded gamely but not quickly enough. The big car had slammed into her Mini just behind her seat, slewing the car almost broadside, and now her foot was jammed down hard on the brake pedal as she struggled to avoid a collision with the bank.

She hit it before she could save herself, and although the seat-belt saved her from injury, her head snapped back with the impact and again the sound of impacting metal made her wince. The engine stalled and then suddenly there was only the sound of her car radio, seeming very loud, blaring out a tune which she could not, for the moment, identify. She sat very still, shocked, listening to the music, before she realised that she had not turned the ignition off, and as she did so she recognised the old song 'Oh, what a beautiful morning' from *Oklahoma*. With a flash of anger she reached over and snapped the radio off, but her fingers shook and she took a deep breath to try to steady herself.

'Get out of there!' The warning cry was unnecessary, she was already unclipping her safety-belt and scrambling clear of the car, aware that she should have got out straight away and angry with herself for not realising at once that she might be in danger.

She stood midway between her car and the white one, which she hazily recognised as being a Rolls-Royce, staring at the Mini and aware that her legs were trembling and that she felt vaguely sick. Hearing footsteps on the road, she turned her head to see that the passenger in the Rolls-Royce had got out and was walking towards her. She took a deep breath to try and control her jangling nerves, and then turned on her heel to face him.

'We'll pay for the damage,' the man said abruptly as he reached her, 'send the bill to this address.' He held out a card and as she took it automatically, he turned away.

'Just a minute!' Kate found her voice and spoke sharply. 'Where do you think you're going?'

'What?' The man turned back to look at her.

'Is that all you're going to say? You could have killed me! Aren't you going to ask if I'm all right?'

'You sound all right,' the man observed.

The callousness of his answer stung her to anger. 'I don't believe this!' she said incredulously. 'You came out of that side road without stopping. I didn't have a chance. How dare you be so casual!'

'I've said we'll pay for the damage,' the man pointed out.

'Well, that's not good enough! I don't even know why I'm talking to you. You weren't driving the car.'

She stalked across the gap that separated the two vehicles, and the driver of the Rolls-Royce opened his door and got out.

'I'm sorry,' he said quietly. 'Are you all right?'

'No, I am not all right!'

'Shall I call an ambulance?'

'Don't be ridiculous!' she snapped, feeling that her anger was threatening to turn to hysteria. She took a deep breath and said more quietly, 'Try calling the police. You shouldn't be on the road!'

'There's no need for that.' The second man came up behind her and now there was a placatory note in his voice, but Kate felt momentarily threatened standing between the two of them.

'There's every need,' she retorted, swinging round to face him. 'I could have been killed! He shouldn't be on the road!' She was repeating herself and she knew it—knew too that her voice had risen dangerously and that she was losing her self-control.

'Look ...' now the man who had been a passenger sounded worried, '... we'll pay for the repairs to your car and any costs you may run up. Hiring another car ... having this one towed in ... whatever.'

She would not cry in front of them. She took a deep breath and said more calmly, 'I see you have a telephone in your car. May I call my garage?'

'Of course.' The driver stood aside and allowed her to sit behind the steering wheel, walking away from his car as she punched out the number automatically, realising suddenly that she still remembered it after more than two years. She relaxed against the upholstery, grateful for the chance to sit down before her trembling legs gave way, and studied the two men as the number rang.

They stood with their backs towards her, looking at the damage to her car and talking quietly, their heads close together. In their denim jackets and jeans she realised that she was not sure which was which. They looked startlingly alike with their thick blond hair, cut in the same style, and their identical height.

The garage promised to send someone out straight away to tow her car in, but the man who answered the telephone was a stranger, so she did not have to endure questions from Jimmy Bell. That would come later, and she hoped that by then she would have stopped feeling sick. She leaned her head against the back of the seat and closed her eyes.

'Hey, honey, are you okay?' The driver was standing by the side of the car, and his soft American voice sounded concerned.

'Don't call me "honey".' There was no fire in her voice. She knew she sounded bad-tempered, but she was too shaken to care. 'If it wasn't for you, I'd be home by now.'

'I'm sorry,' he said again.

'Yes, so am I.'

Now that Kate could see their faces, they were not as alike as she had at first thought. Superficially they bore a resemblance to one another, but the driver was the better looking man of the two, with a physical attraction that Kate recognised and refused to respond to.

'Can we give you a ride home?' he asked.

She managed a small smile. 'The way you drive? No, thanks, I'd sooner walk.' Brave but empty words, for she could not have staggered five yards and she knew he was not deceived. 'The tow truck will get me back,' she told him.

'We'll wait till it comes.'

'That won't be necessary,' she told him quickly, getting out of the car hurriedly. 'I have your card. I'll send you the bill.'

'Come on, we're late as it is,' the other man said impatiently, but the driver hesitated, watching her with blue eyes that saw her sudden nervousness and anxiety for him to be gone, and not understanding her reasons. After a few moments he shrugged and held out his hand to her.

'Thanks,' he said quietly. 'You could have called the police. I'm grateful to you.'

Kate took his hand. 'I'm sure you are,' she said quietly.

'Is there nothing I can do? There's luggage in your car . . .'

'Yes. I told you I was on my way home.'

'You've been away a long time?'

'Yes,' she answered shortly, wanting him to go, not wanting him to meet Jimmy Bell, and to make it quite clear that she did not seek his company she stalked past him to her car, ignoring the other man, to reach for her handbag from the passenger seat. Walking to the bank, she sat down and lit a cigarette, blinking as the smoke drifted in front of her eyes, and then she hugged her knees with her arms and watched dispassionately as the Rolls-Royce slipped carefully around the back of her car and accelerated gently away, annoyed to see that the damage to the big car was only superficial.

The lane was very quiet then, with only the

songs of the birds to keep her company. She laid the side of her face against her knees and hunched her shoulders disconsolately, staring at her wrecked car and suddenly wishing she had not come back. Somehow the accident seemed to be a bad omen, and although she would not admit to being frightened, even to herself, she felt chilled by the realisation that she could have been killed. .

The shadows were deep in that part of the lane, the dense green foliage shielding the sun from her, and she shivered suddenly in her thin cotton blouse and hugged her arms more tightly around her knees, looking beyond the car up the lane along which Jimmy must come.

When he did come, it was the same battered truck that he had been driving around in two years ago, for she immediately recognised the distinctive black paintwork with the yellow side flash, and stood up to greet him as he stopped on the other side of her car.

'Kate!' He leaned out of the cab to stare at the Mini. 'Did you do this all by yourself, or did you have help?'

She opened her mouth to answer him indignantly, but with a grin and a wave of his hand he drove past her to turn the truck around, and when he came back she watched him climb out and walk around the car towards her.

'Welcome home!' There was a big smile on his face and Kate felt herself relax under the easy grin. There was something so comforting and so reliable about Jimmy. 'I'd give you a hug, but I'd spoil your clothes.'

She looked down at her cream blouse and tan skirt.

'It isn't my favourite outfit,' she said mildly.

'Oh, Jimmy, it is good to see you!'

He still hesitated, but she smiled radiantly and suddenly he stepped forward and embraced her in a bear-like hug, the odours of oil and petrol from his garage drifting into her nostrils. So well remembered, that smell of the garage, and those arms that had been hugging her for years. Suddenly she felt safe—protected by his strength and solidness, unutterably reassured by his familiar presence and his acceptance of her. For the first time she felt she had done the right thing in coming home.

'I'm glad you're back, love,' he said softly, and she tightened her arms around his neck, closed her eyes, and pressed a kiss into his neck. She was so grateful to him. Of all her friends, who would give her such an exuberant and wholehearted welcome?

'So . . .' he released her but kept her hands within his as he stepped back a pace to look at her, '. . . the wanderer's returned at last. You look pale.'

'So would you if someone had just smashed into your car,' she retorted. 'Oh, Jim, you've not changed one bit!' And she felt relief sweep through her body. Jimmy would always be a familiar anchor on which she could rely.

With the Mini hooked up to the back of the tow truck and Kate in the front seat, they set off for the village, and Kate listened happily to Jimmy's account of his life during the past two years and cajoled him, without much difficulty, into hiring her one of his cars.

She swayed towards him as the truck rounded a bend and then smiled involuntarily as she saw the garage on the very edge of the village and they passed the sign that said 'Toggleton'.

'Home at last!' Kate arched her back away from

a spring that was digging into her spine. 'From Clare's letters, nothing's changed.'

'Not much,' he agreed, 'but then nothing ever does. I like it that way. Do you want me to drop you at your door?'

'No need. I'll enjoy the walk from the garage.'

He stopped the truck and she jumped lightly down, casting a last rueful glance at the crumpled Mini. Jimmy had promised to give it priority, but it would still be a while before she saw it again.

'I'll bring that Triumph round as soon as I've gone over it for you and filled it up,' he told her. 'Couple of hours be all right? I'll bring your luggage, too.'

'That's fine. Thank you, Jimmy.'

Kate went slowly down the lane, hands in the pockets of her skirt and her handbag slung over her shoulder as she looked around her. The big elm tree opposite the garage had gone. Kate could see the high stone wall that hid the little school she and Clare had attended and, adjacent to the wall, Miss Mole's tiny cottage with its thatched roof. Fifty yards further on, the narrow road divided to circumvent the triangular green that was the centre of village life, and she knew that when she reached it and swung to the right, she would see again the white-painted cottage that was her home. Suddenly she was impatient to be there, to be surrounded by familiar belongings, to feel secure. She kicked at a stone and began to walk faster.

The bright red Cortina parked outside her front gate made her frown for a moment, but the number-plate was as familiar to her as Jimmy Bell's face had been, and the frown became a smile of anticipation. She slipped up beside it, trying to keep in the driver's blind spot, then banged on the

roof with the flat of her hand before bending down
to peer through the driver's window.

An indignant face glared at her, but then the
cross expression melted into a grin of pure delight
and Clare Harroby pushed open her door and slid
out of the driving seat.

'At last!' she said. 'I was beginning to wonder if
you'd got lost. I've been waiting for ages. Miss
Mole's got my key.'

'Aren't you going to welcome me home?'

'Welcome home,' Clare said promptly. 'Now
please will you open up and make me some
coffee?'

Kate turned to look at the house with a loving
eye. It was stone with a slate roof and its plainness
was softened by the honeysuckle that wound its
way upwards around the white-painted windows,
and by the tubs of flowers on each side of the front
door. Lavender bushes and rose trees crammed the
small front garden, vying for space with her other
favourite flowers, but there was not one weed in
sight. Miss Mole had kept her promise to look
after it.

'Coffee?' Clare asked again, plaintively, and
with a laugh Kate led the way up the short path
and unlocked the front door.

Inside, the small, square, white-painted hall was
cool and welcoming. Kate opened the door to her
left into the living room and stepped inside to look
around.

'Home, sweet home!' She stretched her arms
above her head and laughed. 'Why did I stay away
so long?' Her glance fell on the bowl of flowers on
the small Georgian dining table that her mother
had been so fond of, on the roses on the
windowsill, and then on the big arrangement of

flowers in the hearth. Now she knew why Miss
Mole had borrowed the key. She smiled, touched
by the gesture.

'It'll have to be instant coffee!' Clare called from
the kitchen. 'You don't have any for the
percolator.'

'Fine,' Kate called back, but her voice was
abstracted as she wandered around the room,
touching the rosewood upright piano that was a
legacy from her grandmother, the antique carriage
clock that she had picked up in an auction, her
bookcase and her few pieces of silver. Nothing had
changed. It was as though she had never been
away.

Her friends in the village had taken good care of
the cottage in her absence. She could have been
away for two days instead of almost two years.
Even her late father's carefully carved wooden
chess set sat on its board all ready to be used. Yes,
she was home.

The room was light and airy, despite its low
ceiling, and ran from front to back of the cottage.
Kate went over to the french windows to look out
over the tiny, high-walled, paved garden, but at
Clare's call she went back through the hall into the
small modern kitchen at the back of the cottage.

Clare's fair hair swung over her face as she
measured coffee into the twin brown pottery mugs,
and it was such a familiar sight that Kate paused
to watch her affectionately for a moment before
saying softly,

'Thanks for keeping me in touch with the
village.'

'That's okay. I'm not the world's best cor-
respondent, but I do try. Anyway ...' with a
sideways grin, '... what are friends for?'

Kate smiled. Theirs was such a long friendship that had begun even before they both arrived for their first day at the village school under the strict vigilance of Miss Mole, and had survived ever since, despite periods in their lives where job hours, when Clare was training to be a nurse and Kate was working for a local newspaper, meant that they met less often than they would have liked.

Kate's parents had been killed in an air crash just two months after her first novel was published, and their farm on the outskirts of the village was sold, but it was not until after the publication of her second novel that she had given up journalism and bought the cottage in the centre of Toggleton, less than two miles from where Clare now lived as the wife of the local doctor.

It was just before Kate had her third novel published that she had met Miles, and their romance had flourished in the months that he was in England and not travelling abroad for his company. Kate had never told Clare what had gone wrong between her and the man everyone expected her to marry, but she had left precipitously for Vienna and then Paris, and Miles was never mentioned again.

Miles. Kate stared bleakly out of the kitchen window at her bird table while Clare finished making the coffee and seemed content with the silence. Why was she thinking about him now? He had been out of her mind for months, but the memories were starting to return again, and with them the feelings of anger—anger that she knew was mostly directed against herself. Her feelings for him were dead. She made an effort to bring herself back to the present.

'We've had some excitement in the village,'
Clare told her as they walked into the living room
and sat down. 'There's a film being made a couple
of miles from here.'

'Oh yes? Who's in it? Anyone I'd know?'

'Someone called Luke Arran,' Clare told her.
'Do you know the name? He had two or three hit
singles a few years ago.'

'Yes, I do. I didn't know he was an actor.'

'I don't suppose he is, but you know what it's
like . . .' Clare shrugged, '. . . actors want to sing,
comedians want to play Shakespeare. I expect it's
another variation. He and his lady co-star and
various other people have rented Pike House.
They've got guards around it and a couple of
dogs—it's like Fort Knox! And we get young girls
wandering around the village looking for the
house. I suppose he needs the protection.'

Kate nodded ruefully, recalling the face of the
man who had been driving the Rolls-Royce. So it
was Luke Arran! She had thought she recognised
him, but had been unable to equate the quiet
parish of Toggleton with an American singing star.
She laughed shortly.

'Just my luck,' she told Clare. 'All those girls
trying to meet him and I have to hit the jackpot!'

'You've met Luke Arran?' Clare stared at her
incredulously, her mug of coffee poised precari-
ously in front of her lips. 'How did you manage
that? Kate, you have all the luck!'

'I wouldn't call it that,' Kate said drily, and
related the story of her accident to her wide-eyed,
horrified friend. When she had finished, Clare got
to her feet and took her empty mug of coffee from
her fingers.

'You should be drinking brandy!' she exclaimed.

'Why didn't you tell me straight away? Katie, you could have been killed!'

'I pointed that out,' Kate nodded, 'with some force. I'm afraid I showed off.'

'I'd have broken his neck!' Clare said angrily. 'Do you want me to pop across to the shop and get a bottle of brandy?'

'No, thanks, but I'd love some more coffee. Didn't you wonder why I was walking?'

'Never thought about it,' Clare admitted, going back into the kitchen. 'Now you just sit back and relax.'

It was pleasant to have someone concerned for her wellbeing. Kate reached for a cigarette and tossed the packet and her lighter over to where Clare was sitting. The other girl rarely smoked but, unless she had changed, she liked a cigarette with her coffee occasionally.

'Look . . .' Clare came back and stood in the doorway of the room, '. . . I can't stay much longer. Mum-in-law's coming this afternoon for ten days and I must get the house tidied up. Why don't you come and stay too? You must be shaken up, even if you won't admit it, and we've got plenty of room.'

'Thanks for the offer,' Kate smiled, 'but I'm fine here, really I am.'

'Well, you know where to come . . .'

They sat and talked for a while, slipping back into the old easy friendship as though Kate had never been away. Clare talked quickly, as she always did, with expressive gestures of her hands, making Kate laugh again and again with her stories of the village people and their gossip, and with her own mishaps. She felt lonely, and the cottage seemed very silent, after Clare had reluctantly gone, after one more unsuccessful attempt to persuade Kate to leave with her.

She went through every room of her home, opening the windows and mentally thanking whoever it was—she guessed it was Clare—who had made up her bed with fresh linen and gone through the place with a duster and vacuum cleaner.

She thought about Luke Arran too, and acknowledged that he had disturbed her. She had sensed a remoteness in him, a kind of detachment, as though she had not existed for him as a person, and once again she conjured up his face in her mind, trying to analyse the attraction that he held for millions of women throughout the world. It annoyed her that she appeared to have made no kind of impression on him, and when she sat down at her dressing table to brush her short, wavy brown hair, she watched her reflection in the oval mirror.

The level grey eyes that looked curiously back at her were full of a bright warmth that could be hidden behind a flinty veneer of coolness. She wrinkled her short, straight nose, and her mouth turned up involuntarily at the gesture above a jaw that she would have said suggested resolution and Clare would have said showed aggression. Laying her brush down with a small sigh, she frowned critically.

'Unremarkable,' she said aloud. 'After the sort of woman he must meet, is it so surprising that he didn't react to you?' She pulled a face at herself and turned away.

Running downstairs, she paused before the door of the one room she had not yet entered, and when she finally stepped inside she felt a twinge of painful familiarity that made her sigh. Her covered electric typewriter sat squarely in the middle of the empty desk, and a grey steel filing cabinet stood in one corner with—a Miss Mole touch—a vase of wild flowers on top. The room was deliberately spartan, she hated distraction when she worked, but the usual urge to write that she had hoped she would feel·when she walked into the room just did not come to her, and she closed the door decisively.

After the noise and bustle of the Paris street below her apartment, the quietness of the village outside her window seemed almost oppressive. Restlessly she lit another cigarette and prowled the room, all her excitement in coming home deserting her as loneliness and depression settled over her like a miasmic veil.

She had chosen this path, she reminded herself sharply. She had deliberately isolated herself from her friends and her own village, and the reasons had seemed good enough at the time, although now they were less clear with the passing of two years.

Miles. It had been Miles who had made her restless with his talk of Europe and the East and with his avowal that she was too parochial and too unsophisticated. It was also Miles who had given her the impetus to go after their last bitter quarrel.

She would not think of Miles. It still hurt.

Her eye was caught by the top shelf of her bookcase where, in amongst the Dickens and the Dornford Yates, were five hardback and five paperback books. She took out the nearest one, looked at the title for a moment, then turned to the back. Her own face smiled up at her and she studied it dispassionately for a moment before picking up its paperback counterpart. She held one book in each hand, almost as though she was weighing them, her expression contemplative. Then, suddenly and violently, she hurled the paperback across the room, where it hit the piano keys with a discordant jangle then fell to the floor.

'No,' she said aloud, finally and definitely, 'that's all over now.'

Everything was over. Her ability to write had gone and Miles was gone. The fun and challenge of living abroad had palled, and so had the desire to see new places. So she had come home. To start her life again.

CHAPTER TWO

THE hamlet of Toggleton dozed in the heat of the sun, quiet and content in its backwater, wanting no part of the busy main road that ran three miles to the east, and secure in the knowledge that few people bothered to follow the signs that would lead them to the heart of the village.

Yet Toggleton was not completely insular. Newcomers to the village were welcomed by their closest neighbours and visited by the vicar and the vicar's wife, but after that they were left to find their own level. Very few chose not to join the community to some extent, and Toggleton absorbed its newcomers without even the hint of a ripple on the placid surface that it showed to the world.

Kate decided to cook a meal for herself in the evening, and in the early afternoon she stepped out into the sunshine, not bothering to lock her front door. In Toggleton, nobody locked their doors. She strolled slowly across the village green, swinging her basket idly and looking around for familiar faces, but the village seemed even quieter than usual. The children were on holiday from school and she guessed that many families were away, but in the village shop, which was also a post office, she was greeted with pleasure and surprise by the owner and the two customers who were chatting as they bought their stamps and groceries. She lingered amid the scent of polish and crowded shelves, buying more than she meant

to for the sheer pleasure of hearing the gossip and
the feeling of being drawn into the community
again. It was a warm sensation of belonging that
she had missed.

She arranged for papers and milk to be
delivered and strolled back to the cottage, meeting
more people that she knew and content to stand
and chat and enjoy the heat of the sun on her
back. She could almost physically feel the pace of
her life slowing after the frenetic bustle of Paris
where it had seemed important to fill every waking
moment of the day. In Toggleton people had time
to stop and talk, and Kate found the change
refreshing.

The basket of red roses in her porch was large
and very impressive. She eyed it with a frown,
wondering who could have sent it. Niall? As her
agent he would be more likely to send her a ream
of typing paper with a terse note telling her to use
it, and if he had to send her flowers, a single
orchid would be more his style. Yet who else knew
she was here? She discounted Clare, and Jimmy
Bell, if he thought of it at all, would send roses
from his own beautifully kept garden.

She opened the front door and with her basket
of shopping in one hand and the basket of flowers
in the other, struggled through into the kitchen
where she put her groceries away before turning
her attention to the roses.

There was no card, no mention of who had sent
them, but she suspected Luke Arran. It would not
be too difficult for him to find out where she lived,
and he could have seen her damaged car at the
garage. Yet either he or his friend must have acted
swiftly, for the nearest florist was miles away and
she had not been home for many hours.

She had knocked one of the blooms in her search for a card, and now it lurched drunkenly to the left, spoiling the symmetry of the arrangement. Kate decided that it was an improvement, disliking its stiff formality, and impulsively she tried to rearrange the flowers to look more natural until, impatiently, she gave up the struggle and tidied them as best she could.

Where was she to put them? The fireplace seemed the ideal spot, but she preferred Miss Mole's arrangement, and would not dream of hurting her feelings by moving it. There were flowers in the kitchen and flowers in the study, and a small posy on her hall table, but the hall seemed the most logical place, so she carried the basket through, and although it dwarfed the small table, it was effective against the background of the plain white wall.

As she prepared her meal, the thought of not knowing who had sent her the flowers annoyed and exasperated her. She did not like mysteries, and she could not understand why there was no card to tell her who they were from. 'Unknown admirer,' she said to herself as she shelled peas, then she made a face as she realised that she had spoken aloud. It was a habit she had got into lately, and she did not like the implication that she had to resort to talking to herself for lack of company. Yet she knew she had no one to blame but herself.

Yet what choice had she had? The village had been waiting to dance at her wedding to Miles, despite the fact that she had not even been engaged to him. When the final, bitter parting had come from the man she had thought she loved, she had not been able to face the idea of making explanations to everyone. How could she possibly expect anyone to understand the subtle way in which he had undermined her confidence, or to believe that the man they all declared to be charming had a streak of cynicism and ruthlessness that had made her feel oddly claustrophobic?

She had told everyone that she wanted to go abroad to find new locations for her books and to broaden her horizons. It had been an excuse, but it was only now that she could acknowledge that fact.

Jimmy Bell had brought her luggage round half an hour before and had promptly asked her to go for a drink with him that evening at the one public house in Toggleton. Kate had told him she was too tired, but he had been so disappointed that she had agreed to go on her second evening home.

She loved Jimmy. He was the brother she had never had. Unfortunately Jimmy Bell had two sisters and was looking for a wife, and Kate knew that soon she would have to hurt him as she had done once before. She realised that she was walking back into a problem that she had thought she had left behind.

Jimmy had asked her to marry him outside the front door of her own cottage, and she had not known what to say. The words that came so fluently and easily from her pen all tangled up in her head as she tried to explain that she had no wish to marry at all, that she wanted to travel and to be free to come and go as she pleased. She had tried to tell him that she did not love him, not as he wanted her to, but he had misunderstood and had told her gently that he would wait until she was ready to settle down.

'And you were a coward!' she told herself

angrily. 'You hoped he'd find someone else while you were away. And he hasn't.' Again she spoke aloud, and again she was cross with herself, but her relationship with Jimmy was a problem that had to be faced, and the sooner the better. It was not fair to let him go on thinking there was a chance that she would marry him, but she was afraid of saying the wrong thing, of hurting him more than she had to, and of losing his friendship. Absentmindedly she rubbed the back of her neck, which seemed to have gone a little stiff.

As her steak grilled, she tried to put him out of her mind by planning what she would do the next day, her first full day at home. She would see Miss Mole, she would ring Clare and ask her and Michael over for a meal to celebrate her homecoming, and perhaps she would go into Mullbridge or Shersbury and do some shopping. She would have a busy day, then she would go to the Gardener's Rest with Jimmy, and afterwards she would ask him back to the cottage for coffee and tell him the truth as gently as she could.

The coffee percolator was bubbling, and Kate had just finished loading the small dishwasher when she heard her door knocker rap a resonant tattoo. The kitchen clock said eight-thirty. Perhaps Miss Mole had returned from her sister's house and had come to say hello. Kate got out a second matching mug and hurried to open the door, but it was not Miss Mole. It was Luke Arran.

'Oh,' she said, completely disconcerted and aware suddenly that she had no shoes on. He was the last person she had expected to see. 'Hello.'

'I've come to see if you're all right,' he said quietly.

'I'm fine,' she said lightly, 'but thanks for asking.'

'I didn't like leaving you,' he told her, making no move to go, 'but I didn't think you wanted me to stay.'

'I didn't,' she agreed. Standing on the doorstep she was almost his height, and she looked into his face and saw a mixture of concern and wariness and indecision.

'Would you like some coffee?' She had not meant to ask him in, and was surprised by her own invitation.

'Well, thanks.' He sounded as surprised as she felt.

Kate looked over his shoulder at the white Rolls-Royce parked at her gate, and at the other fair-haired man at the wheel.

'What about Tweedledum?' she asked.

'I beg your pardon?'

'Your driver.'

'Oh.' He looked both enlightened and amused. 'I'll tell him to come back in half an hour or so, if that's okay with you.'

'Fine.'

He went back to the car, and she left the front door open while she hurried into the kitchen to get out her coffee cups. Then she changed her mind, put the pretty china away and reached again for the matching pair of mugs. Then she dithered, cursing herself for thinking that Luke Arran might be affronted by being offered a mug. What did she care what he thought? He was just the man who had damaged her car, and he was lucky to be asked in at all.

Luke Arran. Singer-turning-actor. She had enjoyed his records, but what did she know of the man?

Clare had gossiped about him during their conversation earlier that day, but Kate did not know how accurate her friend's information was. She had been told that he was thirty-five and single, with his interests, according to magazines, being golf, tennis and music. At least, Kate reflected, they could talk about music. From what she remembered of the conversation, he had only come to the notice of the public about four years ago with a romantic up-beat ballad that had shot to the top of the record lists. Several other successes had followed, but Kate was sure she also remembered Clare telling her that the man had worked for years to get that first break.

The casual jeans he had been wearing earlier in the day, and the black cords that he was wearing now, were oddly at variance with the gleaming white Rolls, but the soft black sweater that he wore now, emphasising his striking blondness, was expensive. Intriguing mixture of a man, Kate decided.

'What are you doing?' He had moved so quietly that she had not heard him come into the kitchen, and she realised that she must look odd standing there with a cup in one hand and a mug in the other.

'I'm just deciding which to use,' she said casually. 'Which would you prefer?'

'A mug, thanks.' He propped himself up against a cupboard and asked curiously, 'Why did you call Tony Tweedledum?'

'Because I don't know what his name is, and he looks something like you.'

'His name was on the card he gave you this morning.'

'I couldn't remember it. It was A. J. something-or-other. It could have been Andrew, Aaron ...' Kate tried to think of other christian names and her voice trailed off.

'Arthur, Albert,' he suggested. 'Alfred, Augustine ...'

'All right!' she protested laughingly, 'I won't play the name game with you.'

The atmosphere of unease lifted as he laughed with her, and Kate's own wariness abated as she put biscuits on to a plate and then found a tray to carry everything.

'I'll take that,' he told her, and then he was standing by her side and she felt dwarfed by him in her bare feet and vaguely threatened by his presence. Silently she led the way into the living room.

The curtains were closed, the wall lights and the two ivory-shaded lamps glowed softly, enhancing the sheen of the dining table and the piano. The chintz-covered chairs and the settee looked comfortable and homely, and Kate felt a sudden rush of affection for her room.

Luke Arran set the tray down on a small table and looked around him.

'This is beautiful,' he said softly.

'I think so,' she agreed.

'You're lucky.' He turned to look at her. 'I'd like a room like this.'

A small smile twitched at the corners of her mouth. 'You're Luke Arran,' she said. 'From what I've heard, you could afford to buy not just this cottage but most of the village too. You could have a room like this whenever and wherever you liked.'

'I didn't think you knew who I was.' He

sounded genuinely surprised, and she laughed out loud.

'Of course I know,' she told him goodnaturedly. 'Now please sit down and make yourself at home.'

He glanced around him, then settled in the wing chair while she poured black coffee for him at his request and then added cream to her own, aware the whole time that he was watching her.

'You know me,' he said at last, 'but I don't know you. We saw the tow truck and Tony rang them and asked for your name and address.'

'I should have given you those details when the accident happened,' she confessed. 'I remembered afterwards, but at the time I was too shaken.'

'I don't blame you.' He leaned forward. 'Tell me about yourself, Kate Fisher.'

'There's not much to tell.' She shrugged her shoulders, a little surprised by the way he had suddenly turned the conversation.

'Oh, come on! Anyone who can create a room like this has to be someone special. I could go out and buy all the furniture and all the trimmings, but it still wouldn't have the atmosphere this room has.'

'Of course it wouldn't,' she agreed, taking a seat opposite him in the other chair and crossing her long legs. 'A lot of it came from my parents' house and everything else I've bought piece by piece. The room just . . . happened. Everything means something to me, but I suppose the fact that the cottage is old is an advantage. Some of these things wouldn't look so nice in a newer house.'

She sipped her coffee and eyed him covertly over the rim of the mug as he continued to look about him. The subdued lighting threw shadows on to his face and she watched, fascinated, as he moved his head and the blond hair glinted and shone.

'You're staring,' he said suddenly, and Kate became aware that the clear blue eyes were watching her as intently as she had been watching him.

'I'm sorry.' She refused to be disconcerted and she smiled. 'It's just that I've never met a superstar before.'

She wondered if he would realise that she was teasing him gently, and his grin of amusement told her he had a sense of humour.

'I'm no superstar,' he told her. 'Just an ambitious singer who got lucky.'

She appreciated his honesty. 'You're making a film around here?' she asked.

'Yes.' He did not enlarge on the subject and Kate wondered why. Perhaps he didn't trust her. He switched his attention to the piano. 'Do you play?' he asked.

'I do, but I haven't touched it for two years. It probably needs tuning.' She turned her head to glance at it and again became aware of a certain stiffness in her neck that accompanied the movement.

'You said this morning you were coming home,' he told her. 'Where have you been?'

She told him about Vienna and Paris and the jobs she had done when her money had run short, and he asked her if she had been to America, revealing his own Californian place of birth. They talked easily after that, both of them having travelled, and Kate found herself relaxing and enjoying the conversation.

He asked a sudden question about the oak beam that ran across the ceiling, and she turned her head to look up at it. As soon as she did so she winced and put her hand up to her neck.

'What's the matter?' he asked at once.

'I've got a stiff neck.' She moved it gingerly. 'I felt it earlier. Must have been sitting in a draught or something.' She rubbed it irritably and winced again when she tried to turn her head.

'You could have hurt yourself this morning.'

'Oh, I don't think so.'

'Let me see.' He rose to his feet in one easy, controlled movement and went around to the back of her chair.

'It's nothing. Don't worry about it.' She spoke quickly, uneasily, but he was already touching her skin and she took a deep breath to control her sudden, inexplicable nervousness.

His fingers were warm and gentle, but she fidgeted restlessly under his touch that was somehow too much like a caress.

'You could have hurt your neck in the crash.' He sounded worried. 'We call it a whiplash.'

'I've heard of it,' she admitted.

'I'll be surprised if you can move your head at all in the morning.'

'Thanks. You really do cheer the patient up!'

'Does it hurt very much?'

'Only when I turn my head.' She tried a slight movement to the left, and this time was ready for the pain it caused. 'It's come on so suddenly,' she explained. 'A little while ago I hardly noticed it.'

'I don't know much about these things,' Luke Arran admitted, but his fingers started to massage the stiff muscles gently.

'Please don't!' she said sharply.

'You're tense,' he remarked, as if he had not heard her. 'You were tense this morning.'

'Is that so surprising?' she retorted tartly,
wishing he would move away but not daring to
turn her head again.

'And you're defensive and prickly,' he continued.
'I wonder why.'

'I don't know you.'

He was silent, but his fingers still stroked the
nape of her neck and she felt an atmosphere of
strain beginning to build up between them.

'Did you send the roses in the hall?' she asked
suddenly, anxious to break the silence that was
becoming slightly embarrassing.

'I got Tony to send them,' he admitted, 'but
they're not right for this cottage.'

'They're beautiful,' she said gently. 'Thank you.'

'I spoilt your homecoming. It was the least I
could do.' He paused. 'And I'm sorry for the
whole thing. Tony isn't usually like that.'

'I didn't like his attitude,' Kate admitted
candidly.

'No, I don't blame you.' Again the slight
hesitation. 'But he did have his reasons. It
wouldn't be the first time someone's . . . engineered
. . . an accident with my car.'

'What for?' Then she laughed. 'Oh yes, I can
guess. Really? Girls do it just to meet you?'

'Something like that.' He looked embarrassed
and a faint tinge of colour crept into his cheeks.
'Stupid, but I've never got used to it.'

Kate held up her hands in mock surrender. 'I
promise . . . I wasn't trying to compromise you!'

'I know that.'

'And I'm sorry I was rude.'

'You had every right to be.' He moved away
from her then to walk over to the piano and she
watched him uncertainly, a little bemused by his

explanation of Tony's behaviour. She was sure he
was telling the truth, but suddenly it made him
seem remote and yet oddly vulnerable. Had he
been afraid she would think him egotistical? 'May
I try your piano out?' he asked.

'Of course.'

He played from memory, snatches of songs,
some of which Kate knew, and she settled back to
listen, aware that he played well, without any
pretension, but with an obvious feeling for music.

'Will you play for me?' he asked, not turning his
head to look at her.

'I'd rather not.' She got to her feet and went to
stand beside him. 'I hate being outclassed and you
play better than I do. Besides, I haven't touched a
piano in two years. Please, play something else.'

She watched his hands as his long, supple
fingers found their way easily and neatly over the
keys, and studied with interest the heavy gold
signet ring on the little finger of his right hand.
She, too, wore a signet ring on the same finger,
and although his was bigger than hers, they were
both the same oval shape, and both had the initial
of their christian name engraved on the flat
surface.

Abruptly he switched from a ballad into
'Chopsticks', and Kate laughed, went to his right-
hand side, and joined in the tune. He played faster
and faster until she lost the rhythm, could not pick
it up again, and took her hands off the keys in
protest.

'You're too good for me!'

'You just need practice.'

'I thought even I could get through "Chopsticks"!'

He tilted his head to look up at her, meeting her

eyes and holding her gaze with a magnetism that she had felt before, but resisted.

'You make me feel very nervous,' she whispered involuntarily. 'I don't know why, you just do.'

'I told you that you were too tense.' His eyes never left her face. 'Somehow you seem very ... fragile.'

'I'm not fragile!' she protested, and the spell was broken as she laughed. 'I'm as tough as old boots.'

'You seem fragile to me,' he insisted, and she looked at him again, not sure that he was not mocking her. But no, the blue eyes were gentle and he was watching her closely.

'I think Tony's arrived,' she said. 'I heard him sound the horn.'

'So did I.'

'You shouldn't keep him waiting.'

'No,' but he made no movement to stand up, and abruptly she turned away from him to look out of the front window.

'May I come again?' Luke Arran asked, and Kate turned in surprise, trying to hide the pain that the sudden movement caused.

'Of course. Whenever you like.'

'Ah, but will you be pleased to see me?'

He really means that, she thought incredulously. He really isn't sure if he'll be welcome.

She smiled at him. 'Yes, I will,' she admitted. 'I'm afraid I haven't been very hospitable tonight, but I've had better days.'

'I can imagine.' He came close to her again. 'If your neck isn't better in forty-eight hours, I'll have a specialist come up from London to take a look at you.'

'I assure you, it won't be necessary.' She laid a detaining hand impulsively on his arm. 'Thank you for being so concerned, but I'll be fine.' It was a nice feeling, having someone worried about her.

He took her hand between both of his and held it tightly for a moment before he raised it to his mouth, and his lips brushed the palm of her hand in a gesture that was strangely and disturbingly intimate.

'Take care,' he said softly. Then he was gone, and as the Rolls slid away silently into the dusk like a giant ghost, Kate was left to stand in the porch and stare after it with a frown of abstraction on her face.

CHAPTER THREE

'IT's no good, I've just got to take a rest!' Kate
walked to the edge of the cliff, then dropped down
on to the short grass, kicking off her sandals and
massaging her feet. 'I should have remembered
that when you say a stroll, you mean a ten-mile
hike!'

'You're just lazy,' Clare retorted. 'You've
always hated walking.'

'True. Very true.' Kate stretched and then lay
back on the grass, making it obvious that she did
not intend to move for a while. Clare sat down
beside her and stared out over the sea, but while
Kate was content with the silence that followed,
she became aware that Clare was fiddling
nervously with her hair and then with the strap of
her sandal before she said suddenly and very
quickly,

'You do know that people are talking, don't
you?'

'People always talk,' Kate said lazily, 'it's a
means of communication.'

'You know what I mean.'

'I do?'

'Yes, of course you do. Don't be obtuse.' Clare's
voice sounded irritable.

'All right,' Kate said wearily. 'I know what
you're going to say, but say it all the same.'

'People are talking . . .' Clare spoke slowly and
seemed to be being very careful to choose the right
words, '. . . about a white Rolls-Royce that parks

outside your cottage some evenings. It doesn't stay long, no more than a couple of hours, and it's always gone by eleven at the latest ...'

'Very respectable,' Kate interrupted drily.

'Oh, very,' Clare agreed, 'but that isn't the point. The point is that it's there. Everyone knows who owns it and everyone is drawing their own conclusions.'

There was another silence. Kate closed her eyes against the brightness of the sun and the gulls screamed above them both, but she was acutely aware of her friend's restlessness.

'All right,' said Clare at last, 'so you don't want to talk about it. Well, I'm not going to interfere ... I wouldn't even if I could. You're a big girl now. Just ... be careful. You'll still be living here after Luke Arran has packed up and gone home to the States. He doesn't have a reputation to consider.'

Kate could not help the hoot of laughter that followed this statement, and as she opened her eyes she saw that Clare was smiling unwillingly too. Yet the warning note was still in her voice as she said quietly,

'It is a small village, Kate. People will talk and you won't stop them.'

'I know.' Kate sat up abruptly. 'If all this was happening in London, no one would give a damn and you wouldn't have to warn me, but I won't let Toggleton stop me doing the things I want to do. Besides ...' she looked directly at Clare, 'I can't stop him coming.'

'Can't? Miss Mole would say there's no such word. You mean you don't intend to stop him coming.'

'That's right.'

Clare seemed to become absorbed with one
particular gull that wheeled and circled overhead.

'You know, you've been on your own too long,'
she said gently. 'Sometimes it helps to talk to
someone else.'

Kate glanced at her sharply, and as she did so
Clare turned her head slowly to meet her gaze
levelly. They had been exchanging confidences,
secrets, since they were children, and Kate knew
that this was the first time she had deliberately
kept her friend in the dark. It was a shock to
realise suddenly that Clare was hurt by her
reticence, and she cursed silently, torn between a
desire to tell her everything and her own natural
inclination to say nothing.

'All right,' she said, 'but there's very little you
don't know. I don't see him all that often, three
times a week maybe, and when he comes we have
coffee and we talk. We've got a number of things
in common, but I really know very little more
about him now than the day I first met him.'

'That,' said Clare positively, 'is weird.'

'No, not weird. He's a very self-contained man,
that's all.'

'At least you don't sound as though you're
getting too involved with him.'

Kate looked at her soberly. 'That's exactly it!'
she said. 'We're not involved . . .' And she had told
Jimmy Bell that same truth when she had declined
his latest offer of marriage and he had asked her if
there was anyone else. She had guessed he was
thinking of Luke Arran.

'Good!' Clare said positively.

'No. No, it isn't good. We sit opposite one
another and we talk, but we don't . . . share . . .
anything. Sometimes I think it's the cottage he

comes to see and not me at all. We discuss films, travel, politics, but he never talks about himself, although he says coming to see me is the only time he ever gets to relax. I think he spends most of his waking time involved with the film. I'd love to go and watch, but apparently it's what they call a closed set and he won't invite me . . .'

Kate broke off as she realised that Clare was staring at her curiously, her head tipped on one side as though she, Kate, was some kind of strange creature that she had never seen before.

'You really mean you just sit and talk?' Clare asked. 'Just . . . talk?'

'That's what I said,' Kate agreed, but she could not quite keep the edge out of her voice.

'I was right before,' said Clare. 'You are weird. You're both weird. You're very attractive and he's very attractive, and you say you have a lot in common, but you sit on opposite sides of the fireplace like . . . like Darby and Joan. In your place, I'd be very annoyed.'

I am, Kate thought, oh, I am. Aloud she said, 'He's very wary of me and I'm wary of him. I really don't think he wants any kind of involvement with anyone at the moment.'

'That's all very well for him,' Clare said quietly, 'but do you want to be involved? I mean . . .' she hesitated, then finished gently, 'it's about time. You put Miles out of your life two years ago.'

It was a blunt statement and it surprised Kate. When she and Miles had parted after that last vicious quarrel, Clare had not asked one question or made one observation about the affair. Kate, even now, did not know how much she knew. She had just been there when Kate had needed her, and it had been Clare who had arranged the

details of the trip to Vienna, helped Kate to pack
and driven her down to Heathrow. Kate had never
been so grateful to anyone in her life before.

Yet now Clare had asked aloud the question
Kate had been asking herself silently for several
days, and it did not occur to her to prevaricate or
avoid the issue.

'I'm not sure,' she said hesitantly. 'I do know we
can't go on the way we are at the moment, at least
I can't. Every time he comes, I'm nervous of
saying the wrong thing ... intruding on his
personal life ... accidentally knocking down some
of the bricks of the invisible barrier he sits behind.
I have the feeling that if I do that then I won't see
him again.' She paused. 'And as for Miles ...'

'... Miles was an arrogant, conceited, pigheaded
...' Kate glanced sharply across the gap that
separated them and saw Clare pull a face and then
finish lamely, '... man.' She shrugged. 'Sorry.'

'It's okay.' Kate was curious. 'I never realised
you didn't like him.'

'Of course I didn't like him. He made you
unhappy, didn't he?'

Clare had a loyalty that Kate had always relied
on and returned, yet now she had an urge to tell
the truth.

'It was six of one and half a dozen of the other.'
She pulled at a blade of grass. 'There was a ... a
spark between us and instead of blowing it gently
into a nice cosy glow, we sort of blew too hard and
got burned. I think we both thought we'd found
what we wanted, but we tried to change one
another to fit the kind of image we both had.' She
looked up and shook her head. 'Profound, aren't
I?'

'You've had too much time to think about it.'

'Maybe,' and she knew she had admitted more to Clare than she intended, and even now she had not told the whole truth. 'Anyway, it's over and done with.'

'I wish you weren't so independent,' Clare sighed. 'Oh,' she added quickly, 'it isn't your fault. It's the way you were brought up. As you were an only child, I suppose your mum and dad wanted to make sure you could stand on your own two feet from an early age. You were never spoiled.'

'No, I wasn't,' but Kate remembered her youth on the small farm and smiled. She had been happy. Then she remembered Clare's earlier comment. 'What's wrong with being independent?' she enquired.

'Nothing . . . except that a lot of men don't like it.'

'You trying to find me a husband?'

'No,' Clare laughed. 'But while we're on the subject of men, what are you going to do about Luke Arran?'

'I don't know,' Kate answered honestly, then she looked directly at her friend. 'I like him very much . . .'

'Like him?'

Suddenly Kate wanted the subject closed. Clare was pushing her too hard and already she had said more than she intended to. She got to her feet.

'It's time we were getting back. We've come a long way.'

'All right.' With the comment Clare accepted the unspoken declaration that she should talk about something else, and they went home discussing other subjects.

It was early evening by the time Kate got back to the cottage and she ate a simple salad before going upstairs to her bedroom. She pulled open the doors of the long, white-painted wardrobe and surveyed its contents with her teeth digging gently into her lower lip.

On Luke's previous visits she had always worn either a simple dress or a blouse and skirt—unobtrusive clothes that were neat and elegant, but quiet. Tonight she wanted the elegance, but she also wanted to be noticed.

The bright blue kaftan with its white embroidery trimmings was not particularly fashionable or even very new, but she loved it and, better still, felt good in it. She brushed her hair until it shone russet under the light and added a touch of her favourite scent. Not too much, just enough to leave a faint hint of perfume behind her as she moved.

Somewhere in her wardrobe were a pair of very high-heeled navy sandals. She searched for them wondering if she could have thrown them away because she so seldom wore them, but after a few minutes she found them, still in their box, and slipped them on.

Originally they had been an expensive mistake, adding four inches to her height, which in turn made her taller than Miles. He had told her, rather irritably, that he did not expect his girl-friend to be taller than he was when he was just under six feet tall himself. Luke Arran was six feet two at least, and Kate felt the extra height would give her confidence.

A little more make-up than she normally wore increased that assurance, and when she was ready she eyed herself in the mirror critically. Then a wry smile touched the corners of her mouth as she realised she was going to feel very silly if he did

not come, and sillier still if anyone else called on
her. That really would give the village something
to talk about!

Downstairs she switched on the music centre,
closed the curtains and tidied up the newspaper
she had discarded casually on to the floor. Then
she hurried to prepare the coffee. Tonight she
wanted everything to be ready so that when Luke
arrived she would not have to spend time in the
kitchen.

Walking back into the sitting room five minutes
later, she was halted in the doorway by the
realisation of what Luke would see when he came
into that same room. She heard the gentle music,
saw the soft, muted lighting, knew what she
looked like in her long blue dress, and in one
sickening moment she realised what he would
think. It made her feel even more sick to know
that he would be right.

It was the classic seduction scene. It had all the
ingredients, and only one vital thing was missing—
her ability to go through with something that she
had not consciously planned. If Luke saw her and
the room it would ruin the fragile, tenuous
friendship that was building between them. It was
little enough, but it was becoming important to
her.

Her immediate reaction was to turn and run,
but habit made her snap off the music and turn
out the lights first. She did not bother with a coat,
did not think of changing her dress, but scooping
up her car keys she closed the front door and fled
down the path, hardly bothering to acknowledge
the greeting of one of her neighbours who was
passing her gate.

The Triumph was a temperamental starter, but

it seemed to sense her desperation and obediently coughed into life the first time she tried it. The gearbox protested as she pushed the lever roughly into first, but then the car was moving down the lane and turning left on to the Mullbridge road.

Kate drove quickly out of the village, past Jimmy Bell's garage, and then swung off to the left, anxious to leave the road she guessed Luke would use to get to her cottage. Instinctively she was heading towards the sea, to her favourite beach, but she realised that she would have to stay there until at least eleven o'clock before she would dare return to the cottage. It was not a prospect she enjoyed thinking about, but she saw no other way. She could not, she dared not, go back until she was sure Luke would not be there. And if he never came again? As she changed into a lower gear to negotiate a sharp bend, her mind refused to answer the question.

The lane she was driving along ended abruptly at a small, grassy parking place for the few people who knew about the beach, and after a moment's hesitation she pulled off her shoes and her tights, locked the car and walked down to the shore, where she stood on the firm, cold sand, just above the line of the tide, her arms wrapped around herself as she felt the chill of the wind from the sea.

With the back of her hand she wiped away the tears that ran down her face in a gesture that was half anger and half shame. She visualised herself standing in her living room, facing Luke and seeing the expression in his eyes. Would he have been amused or contemptuous? Would he have walked away or would he have stayed?

'Kate?'

She froze, and for a moment considered turning and running from him back towards her car, but he was too close, and with a sigh she turned to see him standing three feet away, his face anxious.

'How did you get here?' She was pleased with the calmness in her voice.

'I arrived at your place just after you left—came by the back road. Your neighbour told me which way you'd gone, and I just managed to see your tail-lights on the side road as I was passing it. I had to find out if you were okay.' When she was silent, he asked softly, 'You aren't okay, are you?'

'Please go away.'

'No,' his voice was very definite, 'I won't. Tell me what's wrong.'

'I can't—I can't!'

Kate swung from him to stare unseeingly out over the sea, willing him to turn away and leave her alone. Half an hour ago she had felt assured and confident, but now she knew that she was vulnerable, and she did not dare to let him see her like that.

'You're cold.' She felt him slip his jacket around her shoulders and she huddled into it, grateful for the warmth that came from his body. His hands rested lightly on her shoulders, squeezing them gently and comfortingly, and she sensed that his uncertainty matched her own. 'Don't cry,' his voice was very soft. 'Kate, please don't cry.'

He was too close. It would be so easy to turn around and lay her head against his chest and relax, but that would give him the right to ask why she was upset and to expect an answer.

'I'm all right,' she took a deep breath and tried to speak lightly. 'Really I am.'

'No, Kate, that's not good enough.' Unwillingly
she allowed him to turn her around so that he
could see her face. 'Something ... someone's ...
upset you. Tell me. We can work it out.' He really
meant it! He wanted to help her, and the irony of
the situation made her laugh unsteadily. 'What is
it, babe?' He was drawing her closer, bringing her
within the circle of his arms but slowly, as though
he was afraid she might break away and run from
him.

She did not run. She relaxed and allowed him to
hold her protectively, too tired and too dispirited
to fight any longer against her need to be close to
him.

'I dressed up for you,' she said quietly. 'I turned
the record player on and I turned the lights down.
I wanted you to notice me. I wanted you to talk
about yourself for once, not just to sit and discuss
safe, neutral subjects. But then I lost my nerve and
I ran.' Silence. She did not dare to look up at him
because she was afraid of what she would see in
his face. 'You never talk about yourself.' She
desperately wanted him to understand how she
felt. 'You're always so reserved, and I'm frightened
of saying the wrong thing.'

How could she tell him that she wanted to be a
more important part of his life than just a casual
friend? She could not be that honest.

'Kate ... oh, Kate!' Now she was being held
more tightly against his body, feeling him breathe,
her head against his shoulder. 'Listen to me,' he
said softly, 'I've got a confession to make.' What
kind of confession could possibly make his voice
unsteady with what sounded like a cross between
laughter and ruefulness? 'You fascinate me,' he
told her. 'I love your honesty and your humour,

but your confidence terrifies me. You seem to be so absolutely and totally sure of yourself.'

'Who, me?' Her voice was incredulous.

'Yes, you.'

She looked at him. 'I ran away tonight,' she told him levelly. 'I saw what you would see and I guessed what you would think. I couldn't face you. How about that for confidence?'

'A big zero, thank God.' He smiled down at her. 'I'm glad you're not sure of yourself all the time.'

'My self-assurance is lying in small pieces at your feet,' she told him lightly. 'Don't tread on the pieces or I'll never be the same again!'

She watched his face intently to see if the subtlety of the remark would reach him and knew, from the way he smiled at her, and the way his hand brushed her hair lightly away from her cheek, that it had.

'I want to tell you something.' He put his arm around her shoulders and she turned obediently and began to walk slowly along the beach at his side. 'You were right about one thing—I didn't trust you.'

'But why?'

'Because too many people have made capital out of me.' His voice hardened. 'There've been articles in the papers about me by people I've hardly known. They've said things ... quoted me ... on the basis of one meeting or one conversation. I've had to learn to be very wary of anyone I don't know, and very careful what I say.'

It was a statement of fact, said quietly and without conceit. Kate knew that Luke Arran was a popular, internationally known personality and an eligible bachelor, and she could imagine the kind of stories that would get into the papers. Now she understood his reticence. She stopped walking and turned to face him.

'And now?' she asked quietly. 'We seem to have let our masks slip a little, so can you trust me?'

'Yes.'

They were walking close to the edge of the water, with Kate between Luke and the sea, and one small wave, bigger than its fellows, rolled swiftly and silently up the sand and curled over her feet and over Luke's shoes. Instinctively she pulled away from him to run further up the beach out of reach of the coldness of the water, but when she stopped and looked back, he was standing just where she had left him, looking down at his feet, and the glance of comical dismay that he threw towards her made her laugh aloud.

'The tide's coming in!' she called. 'If you stay there much longer you're going to get more than your shoes wet!'

'I'll just get the water out,' he called back, and then before her astonished eyes he executed a perfect handstand and waved his feet in the air. Kate burst out laughing at the impishness of his behaviour, then clapped encouragingly as he began to walk unsteadily towards her on his hands.

'Come on!' she called, 'just a few more feet!' and then, as he collapsed with a grunt a yard away from her, 'Luke! Are you all right?'

He lay flat on his back on the sand, spread-eagled and still, but she suspected a trick and kept her distance until finally she could bear it no longer.

'Luke!' She ran to his side and dropped to her knees beside him in a flurry of long skirts. 'Luke, if you're pretending, I'll . . .'

'You'll what?' Luke opened an eye and grinned at her. 'Did I have you worried?'

'Not in the least.' She smiled down at him, loving his ability to be silly and a little crazy, but she added warningly, 'The sand's wet. Get up or you'll catch a chill.'

She stood up herself, and he stared at her feet.

'You've got no shoes on,' he told her.

'I'm aware of that,' she said drily, 'and my feet are frozen. Let's go back to the cars.'

'Right.' In one swift, easy movement he stood up, and in a second unexpected movement, he scooped her into his arms.

'Put me down!' She was shaken by his action. 'Luke, I'm far too heavy for you!'

'No, you're not,' he said easily, and she gave up arguing, sliding her arms around his neck to make it easier for him to carry her and resisting the impulse to lay her cheek against his.

'You feel cold,' she told him. 'Cold and damp. I've got a rug in the car . . .'

'Stop being so practical!' He was walking up the sand, taking his time and holding her tightly. 'I'm enjoying this.'

'Me too,' Kate agreed immediately, then felt her cheeks burn.

'Oh?' He reached the cars and set her lightly on to her feet, keeping one arm around her waist. 'You like the masterful approach?'

She hesitated, trying to find an answer that would keep their mood on a lighthearted level, and then it was Luke's turn to laugh at her.

'Hey!' she said softly, 'be careful—that's my confidence you're standing on!'

'Katie.'

She looked up at him then, and drowned in the fire and ice blue of his eyes. Half hypnotised, she allowed him to draw her closely against the long, lean length of his body, then he bent his head and kissed her.

His mouth was gentle, almost tentative on hers, and she cradled the back of his blond head with her hands to bring him closer to her and show her own willingness for the embrace. It was the kiss of two new, rather uncertain lovers, and it was not until she said his name against his lips very softly that he held her more tightly and the kiss became more passionate and more demanding.

With the kiss their relationship moved on to a different plane, and as he drew back a little and then kissed her again, seeming not to be able to resist her, one small part of Kate's brain was warning her not to go too fast, not to get too involved, but as his mouth lingered on hers, she realised that it was already too late. She did care for him, and her attraction was based on his concern for her. It was a dangerous combination to Kate, who had been alone for so long.

She did not demur when he suggested taking her home in his car, and was content to allow him to promise to have her vehicle returned in the morning, enjoying the feeling of having someone else making the decisions. When he opened the door of the Rolls-Royce for her she sat sideways on the seat and rested her head against the upholstery, realising suddenly that she was tired.

'You've got sand on your feet.' He knelt in front of her to brush it away, and then his warm hands enclosed one foot. 'And you're cold,' he added.

As he looked up at her, the moonlight turned his hair to the colour of ripe corn, and dramatised the planes and hollows of his thin face. Impulsively Kate stretched out her hand and touched the side of his head, lured by the sudden hopeless thought

that soon he would be back in America and she
would be alone again.

'Kate.' He was watching her and now his eyes
were dark and soft. 'You could become very . . .
special . . . to me.'

She was not ready to make such a declaration
yet. She smiled at him and ran a finger lightly
along his jawline in gentle acknowledgement of his
words, and if he was disappointed by her silence
he did not show it.

'You must be cold,' she said softly. 'Put your
jacket on.'

Luke sighed. 'You're like a mother hen!' he
chided her, but she ignored the gentle tease and
slid the jacket around his shoulders.

'I'm practical,' she told him. 'How can you
make a film if you've got double pneumonia?'

'It wouldn't be easy,' he admitted as he tucked a
rug around her, and while she snuggled into it he
went to fetch her shoes from the other car before
sliding into the driving seat of the Rolls-Royce and
turning to smile at her.

The interior of the car was comfortably warm.
She relaxed against her seat and smiled back at
him, subduing the longing to be kissed again and
to cup that fine-boned face between her hands and
caress it lightly. Let him make the moves, she told
herself. Remember Miles? Remember what Clare
said about being too independent and men not
liking it?

'Katie . . .' The changing of her name pleased
her. It created an intimacy between them that had
not been admitted before.

'What?' she asked softly.

'Just . . . Katie.' She was smiling as he drew her
close, and his mouth took hers in a kiss that was

both passionate and infinitely sweet, leaving her breathless and bereft as he drew back.

'There's a party at my house tomorrow night,' he said suddenly. 'I'd like you to come and meet my friends.'

'That sounds fun.' She hesitated, then asked the question that had been in her mind since he found her on the beach. 'What would you have thought if I hadn't run away . . . if you'd seen me in the house dressed like this?'

'I'd have thought you looked very beautiful, which you do. I'd also have wondered if there was to be a seduction.'

'Ah, but would you have gone along with it?'

'Don't be silly!' Luke was smiling. 'Of course I would. I couldn't have resisted you. Maybe you should have stayed at home.'

'Maybe I should.'

Kate dropped her eyes, amazed at her own admission, and she felt a blush heating her cheeks again when she realised that what she had said amounted to a tacit invitation. She had not meant it in that way, and she was not sure he would have the sensitivity to realise exactly what she did mean. Why should he? She was not sure herself.

'I didn't know anyone blushed these days,' he teased her gently. Then, 'It's all right, babe, I'm not going to push you into anything you aren't ready for. What we have is too fragile and too new.'

'I am twenty-six,' she said mildly, 'I'm not a child.'

'And if I suggested going back to your place right now and staying the night, what would you say?'

'I'd say no.'

'Honest Kate!' Luke leaned over and kissed her lightly. 'Do you ever tell a lie?'

'Of course—if it's necessary.'

He started the engine and turned the car around, and Kate relaxed as they began the homeward journey, smiling as he stretched out his hand to take her fingers as they lay in her lap. She was at ease with him now, understanding him a little better, liking him very much more, but still not sure whether she could afford to get too involved. She had been hurt before and she suspected that Luke Arran had the power to hurt her again if she gave him the chance. She was not sure that she wanted to give him the chance.

CHAPTER FOUR

'I HOPE you'll enjoy your evening,' Tony Royal said as he opened the front passenger seat of the Rolls and waited for her to get in.

'Is there any reason why I shouldn't?' Kate was dismayed that Luke had not come to fetch her to the party himself, as he had promised, but she still tried to mask the sharpness in her voice.

'No, of course not.' His face was carefully bland, but she sensed a kind of restrained irritation behind his words. 'But there won't be many people you'll know . . .'

'Oh, I'm sure there will be.' Had he forgotten that she was a native to this area of the country, or was there some other implication behind his words? Or was she reading too much into a casual conversation?

He shrugged. 'Maybe,' and went around to get into the driver's side, while Kate took a deep breath and tried to relax. She had no reason to be nervous. Luke had invited her to this party himself and it was no business of this taciturn friend of his. It was Luke's party. On the other hand, she wished that the first meeting after their closeness of the previous night could have been more private. She would have liked to be alone with him.

She knew little about the man who was driving her to Pike House except that he was Luke's stand-in, doubling for him in the fight scenes and some of the rehearsals where they were setting up

the lighting and Luke himself was not really
needed. She guessed that the two men were
friends, knew that Tony also acted as chauffeur to
his blond counterpart, but none of this accounted
for the sense of hostility that she felt in him.
Hostility towards her.

The party was only a short ride away and she
was glad of the proximity to her own cottage. The
man by her side unnerved her with his silence and
his veiled air of disapproval, but she lacked the
courage to challenge him and break the tension
between them. So she played with the strap of her
handbag, stared out through the windscreen of the
great car, and tried to breathe deeply and quietly
to steady herself.

Pike House had been built since her departure
from the village, but she knew its reputation. It
was called the glasshouse by the local people, and
as they turned into the drive, she understood why.
It was very large and very modern and she
imagined it would have looked quite in keeping
with the houses of film stars in the hills around
Hollywood. In its present setting it looked totally
out of place.

Luke was not there to greet her at the door.
Kate was led through the house, too bemused by
all the people there and the brightness of the
rooms to take note of anything but the sheer
opulence of the place, but resentment crept in
swiftly as Tony found her a drink and stayed
obdurately by her side, not seeming to want to
talk, but introducing her dutifully to different
people and then moving her on before she could
get into conversation with them.

Her writer's mind, ever alert for situations that
she could use, should have found rich pickings at

Pike House among the people who thronged the gardens and clustered around the big swimming pool under the coloured lanterns and the natural light of the clear moon, but she was too concerned with the strangeness of the situation to make mental notes.

Why half of them had been invited at all was a mystery to her. She suspected that many of them were the extras who had been recruited from Shersbury, but she also recognised some of the people who lived close to Pike House, and they seemed slightly ill at ease in the company in which they found themselves. Some of the local farmers were there too, drinking champagne and seeming happier in their surroundings, but it was a strange mixture of people and on any other occasion she would have found the situation intriguing.

Tony finally seemed to get bored with the introductions. Kate found herself being steered down the garden to the side of the big swimming pool. It was quieter here, but that very quietness once again emphasised the tension between herself and the man by her side. She turned to him.

'Where's Luke?' she asked.

'He'll join you as soon as he can,' Tony told her, and she wondered if she was imagining the evasive note in his voice, or the feeling that she was deliberately being kept away from the main body of guests.

'Let's go back to the lawn,' she suggested, wanting to test him, and sure of her suspicions when his hesitation gave him away.

'You must be Kate!' A tall, angular man in his fifties hurried towards them and introduced himself as Ray Robbins, Luke's manager, and as Tony drifted discreetly away, he took her arm with a familiarity that made her eyes narrow imperceptibly and her instincts warn her to be on her guard.

'Luke's told me all about you,' he said conversationally.

'Really?' She was carefully noncommittal.

'He has a very high opinion of you.'

'Oh yes?' She maintained her pleasant, neutral tone, determined to give nothing away.

They were walking away from the pool back towards the house, and suddenly she saw Luke ahead of her, in a group of people, a glass in one hand and a long, thin cigar in the other. He looked relaxed, and the girl with hair the same colour as his own who clung possessively to his arm, laughed and tossed her bright mane of hair as she listened to him talking.

'That's Sandy Gale,' Ray told her quietly. 'Luke's co-star. I expect you recognise her. They make a good couple don't they?'

'She's very pretty,' Kate acknowledged, evading the question, her eyes raking over the slim figure in her bright red dress.

'They have a lot in common,' Ray told her. 'It's a very ... close ... relationship.'

'Really?' Schooled uninterest now, although she understood the implication behind the carefully chosen words and could not prevent her body stiffening with shock at the revelation.

'Oh, sure,' Ray said easily. 'You know, Luke will be a big star soon. He's got what it takes. And Sandy ... well, Sandy knows the business and she'll help him. She knows about good publicity and she won't mind if Luke has to escort another lady to a premiere or be seen around with other girls. The Press in the States like to think they've discovered a new romance and, like I said, it's all publicity. Mark you, he has to be seen with the right people.'

Those last few words were the important ones, and while Kate doubted that Sandy Gale would be as understanding as Ray seemed to think she would be, she realised that, to Ray, she was not one of the 'right people'. She said nothing.

'Of course, Luke has a lot of girl-friends.' The man spoke quietly, insidiously. 'But he and Sandy ...' His voice tailed off, but he did not need to say any more. The message was quite clear. She was being warned off, and her temper rose at the audacity of the man who stood by her side.

Staring at the group, not wanting to look at the man who was forcing her to see Luke Arran in an entirely new light, she said casually,

'Really, Mr ...' she let her voice trail off as his had done, although she remembered his name perfectly well, 'I know all about Sandy.' Liar! some inner voice said mockingly.

'I just didn't want you to think ... to hope for ...' Now he floundered, and she turned her head swiftly to look straight at him.

'To hope for ... what?' she asked coldly.

'You know what I'm talking about.'

'Do I?' she parried. 'Well, Mr ...' again she chose to forget his surname, 'I'll tell you this. I don't take kindly to people meddling in my life. I don't like you and I don't like what you're saying, so if you'll excuse me ...'

'You won't hold him.' His voice caught her attention as she turned away, and she swung back to face him. He spoke so confidently, so positively, and she could not resist the implied challenge. 'At the moment you're a novelty,' he said softly. 'Someone different. But it won't last.'

His conviction shook her, but she fought against letting him see that she was disconcerted, and after a moment of panic when her mind refused to work, anger caused adrenalin to flow and her brain formed the words to cut him down.

'You're forgetting one thing,' she spoke quietly, almost gently. 'You're assuming that I want to hold him. Actors do have a reputation for being insecure and ... well, a little strange sometimes.' Luke would kill her if he heard about that! 'I'm not going to spend my life boosting his ego and standing in the background so that he can shine. I have my own career and I'm not at all sure that I need an American film star ... singer, whatever he calls himself these days ... to complicate it. I have my own reputation to consider.'

Before he could answer she was walking away from him, moving straight-backed across the lawn away from Luke towards a group of people whom she knew slightly, joining them with a smile and word of greeting and content to stand and listen to their conversation while her heart hammered and her fingers trembled. Yet her anger still simmered, and she tried to quench it with the assurance that she did not need Luke Arran, that he was just a pleasant interlude in her life, that he was no more than a casual affair. Then she angered herself even more with her own self-deception and cursed the day that he had driven into her car.

'Kate! Hey, Kate!' He was calling her, and she turned towards him as he hurried over the grass to her. 'I've been looking for you.'

'I've been here.' And he hadn't been looking for her.

He reached her side and she expected him to kiss
her. When he just put his arm around her waist
and hugged her lightly for a moment, she felt
cheated.

'How are you?' he asked her.

'Very well, thank you.' She would not claim him
with a hand on his arm as Sandy had done, but
she wanted him to show the others that they were
more than just casual friends.

'Ray wants me to meet some people,' he told her
quietly. 'I'll get back to you in a few minutes.
Okay?'

This was not the way she had expected the
evening to go. He had invited her and she did not
expect to be left alone while he squired Sandy Gale
around the garden. Then, as she looked indignantly
into his face, she saw his own uncertainty, his
silent plea for her to accept what he proposed, and
she sighed.

'All right,' she said placidly, but it was hard to
see him turn away and walk back to Sandy, and
harder still to pretend she did not care when all she
wanted was to be by his side, her hand within his,
sharing the evening with him.

'Hi!' The bright voice made her jump and she
turned from her circle of people to stare straight
into a pair of the greenest eyes she had ever seen.

'Hello.' She was on her guard once again. The
one-word greeting had been enough to tell her
that the redheaded beauty she was looking at was
also an American, and she was becoming less and
less fond of anyone American as the evening
progressed.

'I'm Nancy, Luke's secretary. You must be
Kate.'

'Yes.' She forced a little warmth into her voice,

although one part of her wanted to laugh. Why had she had any thoughts of Luke being any more to her than just a casual encounter? This Nancy was so beautiful with her long, shining hair and her slim elegance. Cynically she wondered if Nancy could type.

'How do you do.' They shook hands, and Kate was aware that her own was damp and hot while the tapering fingers of the other girl were cool. 'Luke's told me all about you.' Nancy smiled.

Another one? Was she the talk of the county?

'Oh yes?' she fenced politely.

'Sure. He's very taken with you.' Nancy turned and Kate found herself walking back towards the house by her side, admiring the other girl's manipulative powers. 'I hear you've had some very cosy evenings back at your cottage.'

'Have you?' How dared he! How dared he go back to his house and discuss their meetings! A great knot of misery settled in her stomach and made her feel vaguely sick.

'Oh, sure. Luke and I don't have secrets from one another. Would you like to see round the house?'

Kate was very tempted to say no and to leave the party before her rising anger made her do something she would later regret. Only the thought of Luke stopped her. Those sapphire blue eyes rose in her mind and she saw again how they had become hazy and soft last night after they had kissed. Was she willing to forgo seeing those eyes again simply because Luke's friends and associates didn't like her?

'Yes,' she said quietly, 'I should like to see the house.'

They toured it slowly, Nancy never missing an

opportunity to demonstrate some gadget or some
feature, and the redhead's enthusiasm for what
Kate regarded as mere gimmickry softened her a
little. The girl was so full of vitality, and seemed so
eager to show her everything, that she found
herself responding to the spontaneous friendliness,
even laughing as they ascended the stairs, and
Nancy gave her a pithy and witty résumé of the
previous owners.

'How about this for a bathroom?' Nancy flung
open a door and Kate stepped inside, to blink in
astonishment. She nearly let her jaw drop, but
recovered in time to stare around in amazement.

'It's incredible!' she said weakly, and she saw her
own reflection shimmer a hundred times over in
the glass-covered walls. The shining navy-blue
sunken bath was huge, the gold fitments of the
taps shone in unremitting splendour, and the
carpet on which she walked was impossibly thick.
She tried to imagine herself in such luxury and
found it impossible, and then tried to imagine
Sandy or Nancy in here. It fitted better, and
suddenly she lost the desire to laugh that the
ostentatiousness of the place engendered in her.
It was showy and she did not like it, but many
other people would. People like Luke and Sandy
and Nancy. Suddenly she felt terribly out of
place.

'Come with me.' Nancy led her out of the room
again, and she was glad to go. Another door was
thrown open. 'This is Luke's bedroom,' Nancy
announced.

No. No, this wasn't fair! Kate cast one hurried,
overwhelmingly curious glance around the cream
and brown-coloured room and stepped backwards.

'I don't think Luke would like this,' she began,

and her voice was pleasingly calm and definite in her own ears.

'Why should he care?' Nancy was behind her and pushed her gently forward again into the room. 'I'm sure he's been in yours.'

It was said so calmly and so reasonably that for a moment Kate did not realise the implication. When she did, she felt the colour rise in her face, and she fought the impulse to round on the other girl and deny the words. What should she say? As with Ray, the words hammered inside her skull in a jumble of meaningless phrases and for a second she was frozen with anger and shock. Then she turned.

'Of course,' she said sweetly, and because it was true the words had a ring of sincerity. He had been in her bedroom, when she had been showing him the cottage, but she was astute enough to know what lay behind Nancy's words.

'Well then,' the other girl shrugged, 'take a good look. The bed's very comfortable.' The redhead's guileless smile made Kate grit her teeth. There was something indecent about the whole conversation and she wanted to escape from the big room with its restful colours and its spartan appearance. 'It's a waterbed,' Nancy added. 'Waveless.'

'Waveless?' Kate echoed blankly.

'Yes—one of the later sort. It's better if there are two people sleeping in it to have this kind.'

'Oh.' She had never seen a waterbed before and she would have liked to look at it more closely, but this was Luke's bedroom and she felt she was invading his privacy. Suppose he found her here? The thought made her go cold.

Nancy was still in the doorway behind her. Kate turned and smiled.

'Excuse me,' she said politely.

'Oh? Seen enough? Well, I should take a good look because I don't think you'll see it again.'

'Oh? Why?'

'Can't you guess?'

'Why should I?' Kate countered smoothly. 'I'm sure you're going to tell me anyway.'

'Because I won't let you. Luke and I . . .' the green eyes sparkled with malice, '. . . well, you English don't like to be too forthright, so I'll wrap it up a little. He's mine.'

'I'm sure he'd love to hear you say that.' Kate wondered if the subtlety of the barbed threat would be lost on the other girl. It was not. She saw the green eyes slide away from hers for a fraction of a second and then return and stare at her coldly. Kate did not think she had ever seen such hostility before.

'Lady, you don't understand what's goin' on here . . .' The suddenly heated words betrayed, for the first time, a hint of a Bronx accent that Kate recognised and she knew that she had, for a moment, upset Nancy's assurance.

'Oh yes, I do,' she said quietly, 'I know exactly what's going on!'

She pushed past the redhead and went back into the passage, finding the stairs and running quickly down them. Luke and Sandy. Luke and Nancy. Luke and Kate. How many other gullible Kates were there scattered around the county? The question inflamed her anger and clouded her judgment temporarily, but her sense of direction remained unimpaired and she slipped out of the front door of the house, cursing the fact that she had not brought her car. The idea of walking did not appeal to her, but she would not return to

telephone for a taxi. If she saw Nancy or Ray or
Sandy or Luke—worst of all, Luke—she would
probably scream and throw something!

The gravel of the long drive hurt her feet
through her thin-soled shoes, and she drew in her
breath in a gasp of pain as her foot slipped and her
ankle twisted over. Footsteps scrunched on the
stones behind her, but she did not bother to look
back. All she wanted was to get as far away from
Pike House as possible so that she could think
and seethe and curse the unkind fates in solitude.

'You aren't leaving, are you?' Luke's voice, and
Kate bit into her bottom lip in anguish before
turning to face him.

'Yes,' she said quietly.

'Why?'

'I don't like your idea of hospitality.'

'Oh yeah? And what d'you mean by that
exactly?' She saw the flare of fire from the end of
his cigar as he drew on it. The deep shadows of the
drive blended with the dark olive green of his shirt
and the black trousers that he wore, and his voice
was quiet and remote. 'Can't say I think much to
your manners as a guest either.' His American
drawl became more pronounced. 'I told you I'd
only be a few minutes. I've been looking for you.'

It wasn't his fault. Suddenly she saw that clearly
and starkly. Ray and Tony and Nancy had
contrived to keep the two of them apart, and to
have gone to that amount of trouble had to mean
something. What? That they thought she posed
some kind of threat? That their golden-haired
goose was in danger of being influenced by an
outsider? Kate did not know.

The flare of temper inside her died suddenly,
leaving her feeling cold and empty.

'I'm sorry,' she said quietly, and then there did not seem to be anything else to say. She would not accuse his friends and would not complain about them to him.

'Yeah, me too.' He drew her off the gravel of the drive and towards the trees that lined its edge. 'What happened? Did someone upset you?'

Oh, but he was perceptive, this blond charmer who had kissed her so beautifully the night before!

'It doesn't matter,' she said lamely. 'It isn't important.'

'Of course it is.' He was so close to her. She could smell the cigar that he was smoking and the subtle fragrance of his after-shave, and she looked up into his unsmiling face and sighed.

'I think I'd better just go home,' she said firmly. Leave him to Nancy or Sandy or any one of the dozens of attractive women at his party!

'No.' He took a deliberate step towards her and she backed away nervously. This was not the big, gentle man who had performed a handstand on a chilly beach, or the quiet man who sat in the living room of her house. This was someone she did not know. 'You aren't going home,' he told her pleasantly, 'until you tell me what's been going on. I looked everywhere for you. I really wanted to enjoy this party with you.'

Kate took another step backwards and saw, in the darkness, the whiteness of his teeth as he smiled. He knew very well that he was making her nervous, and he was enjoying himself. She could feel her heart thudding heavily and the palms of her hands suddenly going damp, and she resented both things. Taking another step backwards to keep the small gap between them, she found her back against a tree, and she knew she was trapped as her fingers reached behind her to touch the rough-grained wood and she realised that it was a big, solid oak. She remembered having admired the trees as they drove up the drive.

'Gotcha!' said Luke softly. 'Now, will you please tell me what's going on?'

She could lie. She could say that she was feeling ill, she could tell him she had a headache, she could find some petty excuse, but he would probably believe none of them. She took a deep, shuddering breath and said calmly,

'I didn't like the way I was being treated.' She could, if pressed, tell him about Ray. She would not tell him that she had been in his bedroom discussing his relationship with his secretary.

'And what the hell's that supposed to mean?'

'It means I've been warned off you,' and the resentment returned again, only this time it was directed against Luke himself. It sounded so silly, put into words, so how could she ever explain to him the humiliation she had felt, which had been doubled after her conversation with Nancy.

'Oh.' Luke did not sound particularly surprised, or even displeased. 'Was it Ray? Don't let him get to you, honey. He's only trying to protect me. You won't be the first lady he's tried to steer away from me.'

Nor the last, Kate thought grimly, and she guessed that Sandy and Nancy would have Ray's approval because they were all a part of the same world. While Luke was with one of them, he was also under Ray's eye.

'Oh yes?' she asked coldly. 'Well, I didn't like it. And if you'd been with me, it wouldn't have happened, would it?'

'No. I'm sorry—guess I thought you could take care of yourself.'

'I can!' His remark stung. She did pride herself on her independence. 'I decided to take care of myself by going home.'

'Without saying goodbye?' He closed that small, safe distance between them and Kate schooled her face into an impassive mask of indifference. She was not sure of him in this mood. She could feel the tension in his body and guessed that under the lightness of his tone he was angry. Yet wasn't she the one who had a right to be angry? She was the one who had been hurt.

'I'm sorry.' That was the second time she had apologised, but she felt she could afford to make the gesture.

'Me too.' Luke sounded a little sad, a little defeated. 'I thought we had something special between us. Last night was . . . beautiful.'

'It was.' The words were out before she could bite them back. 'I just . . .' she shrugged helplessly, '. . . well, I was made to feel I was chasing you. Like some kind of gold-digger . . .'

'I know you're not that.' The assurance in his voice warmed her heart suddenly, and when the index finger of his right hand traced the shape of her lips in a slow and sensual exploration, it was as if a million butterflies had been brought to life inside her. 'I just wish you'd trusted me enough to come and tell me . . .' The finger trailed down her jaw and curved along her throat.

'And I wish you'd trusted me enough to realise that I wouldn't have left without a good reason. I didn't want to complain about your friends to you.'

It was meant to be a calm defence of the way

she felt, but it came out as a plea for his understanding. His finger was curving around her ear now and he had moved fractionally closer so that she could feel the heat from his body against her own. In her high-heeled shoes her eyes were level with the strong, clean line of his neck and throat, and she had to repress a desire to kiss the small pulse that she could see beating there. She raised her eyes to his face and smiled uncertainly.

'Come back to the party with me.' Luke bent his head slightly and kissed her forehead. She sighed. 'Don't you want to?' What should she say? That she didn't like his friends or his house or seeing him surrounded by so many people who demanded his attention? All of it was true. 'I would have come and picked you up tonight,' his lips pressed small kisses along each of her eyebrows, 'and I'd like to spend the whole evening with you. But if I do that . . . well, there are photographers here. They'd get your name and there'd be some kind of story in the papers. I'm trying to protect you from that.'

'I wish you'd told me.'

'Maybe the party wasn't such a good idea after all.' He sighed and moved away from her slightly. 'But how could I not ask you? You would have heard about it and been hurt. And I wanted you here tonight, to be with me.'

It was such a gentle, understated declaration that for a moment Kate did not take in the full implication. When she did, the butterflies woke up again and the darkness took on the texture of thick velvet, suffocating in its intensity. All there was for her in the world at that moment was the rustle of the leaves in the tree above her head and Luke Arran's face as he smiled at her, golden head a pale shimmer in the blackness, eyes that looked solemnly into hers and waited for her to answer his statement.

'Luke . . .' Now, at this moment, they were both vulnerable and uncertain. Kate was not sure whether he wanted her to go or to stay and she felt she was facing some kind of test. '. . . if you really want me to stay then I will,' she began hesitantly, 'but I'm not sure that it's a good idea. I just want you to myself!' She finished with a rush and knew that she could have explained so much better if she had been allowed to write it down. She raised her hands to his shoulders and squeezed them gently. 'It's all so new.' She tried to explain again, but his fingers on her lips stopped the words in her throat.

'I know how you feel.'

'Do you? Do you really?' She was not sure that he did, but she stared at him hopefully and watched his face soften.

'I think so. I'll take you home.'

It was somehow an anti-climax, and yet she was not sure what she had been expecting. Would she have preferred Luke to insist that she stay?

'It's all right.' He must have seen her uncertainty. 'I do understand. You aren't going to be happy here. I'll get the car.'

'No.' She made the decision swiftly. The flatness of his tone had told her the truth. 'I've spent hours getting ready and I'm not going to let your manager, or whatever he is, drive me away. I'll stay.'

'That's my Katie!' His arms crushed her and she felt the hardness and strength of his body as he lifted her off the ground. She laughed aloud with the sheer joy of having made him happy, and then he was kissing her so that there was nothing in her universe but his mouth moving on hers and his hands somehow possessive and claiming, on her back.

She pressed against him in yielding triumph and let her fingers slide into the fine silk of his hair. Nothing mattered, not Ray or Nancy or Sandy or anyone else. For the moment they belonged to one another and nothing else was important. She closed her eyes and clung still tighter, not allowing the doubts and fears that crowded her mind to spoil the moment.

CHAPTER FIVE

THE church clock was striking ten as Kate stared at the paragraph she had been typing on her machine. With her chin in her hands, and her elbows resting on the top of the typewriter, she assessed what she had written, trying to read it impartially as through someone else's eyes. As she did so a corner of her mind was telling her that the day was Thursday and she would be seeing Luke that night. The thought upset her concentration so that she had to start reading the paragraph from the beginning again.

Her door knocker rattled loudly, and she pulled a face and stood up stiffly. It rattled again as she got to the door of the room and the impatient tattoo jangled her nerves.

'All right,' she called crossly, 'I'm coming!' and then, as she opened the door, 'Hello, Luke. I didn't expect . . .'

Her voice, full of warmth and surprise, faded away at the expression on his face, and before she could speak again he had stepped inside the cottage, slammed the door shut and grabbed hold of her wrist as he stalked past her into the living room. Towed along behind him and stunned by the fury in his face, Kate stumbled in his wake until he swung her around to face him in the middle of the room.

'Let go of me!' She found her voice and tried to pull her wrist away, but his fingers were digging into her skin and she could not free herself.

'Look at me!' he commanded, and she stared up at him in astonishment, her grey eyes wide and startled as she saw that his face was etched into lines of furious anger, and his own eyes were as cold as blue ice. Then he cursed, bitterly and briefly, and before she could stop him he was kissing her, his mouth as hard and angry as his face had been.

She struggled for a moment, but behind the passionate fury she sensed a kind of inner despair that caught at her heart and made her respond to him in puzzled tenderness that seemed to infuriate him even more. His kiss became rougher, demanded more, until she gave an inarticulate cry of protest, whereupon he set her free and pushed her away from him.

'What's the matter?' she demanded, taking another step backwards to be out of his reach. 'What's happened?'

'I trusted you.' There was a world of bitterness in his voice. 'I don't know how you've got the nerve to face me.'

'I don't understand,' she told him quietly. 'What's all this about?' She had to calm him down before he did something he would regret. He looked both dangerous and violent, but it did not occur to her to be really frightened, just bewildered.

'As if you didn't know!' He threw a crumpled newspaper towards her that she caught instinctively. 'Centre pages,' he told her. 'They should pay you well for it.'

She leafed through the paper, half guessing what she was going to find, but the headline that caught her eye was still a shock and she had to read it a second time before it sank in.

'Singer in holiday romance,' the headline said in thick black letters. The byline was worse: 'Local girl's own story of love-affair.'

Raising her head, she looked at Luke, saw the distaste and disillusionment that made him look almost ugly, and turned her eyes hastily back to the article, wincing as phrases leapt off the paper to make her feel sick with fury and disgust.

'Rolls always parked at her gate—has Luke Arran fallen for the English rose?' caught her startled eyes. 'Walking on the beach at night with his lady-love,' the paper averred, and then further down, 'Midnight assignations on Pevensey beach.' There was no name at the end of the article, and as Kate stared at it the printed characters blurred before her eyes.

She would not cry! Blinking hard, her teeth gnawing at her bottom lip, she re-read it quickly, and when she had finished she took a deep breath and met Luke's accusing glare steadily.

'If you're thinking that I wrote this, then you're wrong,' she said calmly.

'It's all there, isn't it? Who else was on the beach?'

'I wouldn't know. But I didn't write it. How dare you think I did!'

He was staring at her, his face as incredulous as his voice had been, but she met his gaze levelly, secure in her innocence but heartbroken by the disbelief and hardness that she saw.

'And I called you honest!' he said at last. 'My God, how you must have laughed! Why didn't you wait? In another week or two you might have got an even better story!' Before she could answer, he had slammed out of the room.

'Luke!' Her voice was a small, despairing wail,

but she spoke to an empty house. She ran to the window to see the Rolls-Royce pull away from the gate, and had a blurred impression of Tony's face staring in her direction before the car was gone.

'Oh, Luke!' This time she heard the edge of anger in her own voice, but the room had suddenly gone cold, and she crossed her arms around herself as she turned away from the window to stare again at the offending paper that lay on the floor where she had dropped it. She kicked at it in rage and bitterness, and it tore across the big picture of Luke that had been a part of the article. Somehow it seemed fitting; retaliation for her hopes and dreams which now lay in tatters at her feet. He hadn't listened to her, hadn't believed her, and it hurt more than she would have thought possible.

Who had done it? That was the question that flashed into her mind and stayed there, and it was followed immediately by three names. Struggling for some kind of control over her emotions she tried to be objective. Nancy was the most likely, and then Ray, followed by Sandy. Sandy hadn't actually met her, but Kate had to assume from what Ray had said that she had a proprietorial interest in her co-star. And then there was Tony. What about Tony?

If only it hadn't happened now! Restlessly Kate paced the room, biting into her bottom lip and deliberately standing on the paper each time she passed it. If it had to happen at all, why could it not have been when they knew one another better, when they had more trust and more understanding between them?

Oh, Luke! If only he had asked instead of accused. If only he could have listened! She had not thought he would have such a violent temper,

and she was still stunned by the ferocity of his
verbal and physical attack on her. It was so unfair.
At that moment she hated him as much as she
hated the person who had done this to them. Why
couldn't he have listened to her?

The letterbox rattled and she swung around, a
sudden hope rising in her that made her feel
lightheaded. He was back! He had come to say he
was wrong.

The small white envelope that had arrived by
the second post sat squarely on her doormat. It
was a sharp disappointment, and she ripped it
open impatiently, noting the local postmark.

'Oh no!' She spoke the words aloud and felt the
blood recede from her face as the thick, black-
printed obscenities on the single sheet of paper
wavered before her startled eyes. 'No!' It was a
protest and a denial of what she held in her hand,
and for a moment she leaned against the wall of
the hall and squeezed her eyes tightly shut to try
and block out the ugliness. Her legs would not
hold her up. She slithered down the wall so that
she sat on the floor with her back resting against
it, then screwed the paper up into a tight ball and
threw it away from her with all her strength.

Still the words danced before her eyes. She
could not blot them out. She felt sick and dizzy
and automatically put her head between her knees
to try to stop the overwhelming faintness. She
could not breathe, she could not see, and she could
not have spoken to save her life. What kind of
enemy had she made who could use such vile
language, make such terrible insinuations? Of all
the people that she knew, who would threaten
Luke?

Threaten? Yes, it had been a threat. She

scrabbled across the floor and read the letter again, trying to ignore the hated words to concentrate on just the last few. 'Or something could happen to him.' Kate read each word slowly. By itself, taken out of context, the threat sounded weak. It was only the impact of what was said earlier that made it appear so frightening.

The chill that she had felt after Luke had left had now become the ice of fear. She felt cold right through to her bones and her teeth chattered as she sat on the floor and wondered if she would ever have the strength to get up again.

She wanted to tell someone, to share her horror and her fear, but who? She could not show it to Clare. Her instincts told her that she just could not allow herself to subject her friend to the awfulness of reading it. Luke was the last person she could show it to. What did they say? No smoke without fire? Would he reassure her, but would the seeds of more doubt be sown in his mind? And the letter accused him too. She would not be able to endure the embarrassment of having him read it.

Unsteadily she hauled herself to her feet and went into the kitchen. With hands that shook, she took a dinner plate from the cupboard, put the letter on it and set fire to it. Only when it had been completely burnt and the ashes flushed away down the sink did she lean against the worktop and let her self-control slide away from her again. It was done. It was over. Now she could not be tempted to show it to anyone. She knew she would not be able to bring herself to repeat verbally the foul language contained in it, so there was no fear of her contaminating either Clare or Luke—the two people who she cared most for in the world—in a fit of weakness.

'It's only words,' she told herself aloud. 'Just
words.' She hammered out the reassurance over
and over to herself with eyes closed and teeth
gritted against a renewed attack of trembling. Only
words. Words couldn't hurt her—not unless she let
them. She would not let them. It was only words.

A cup of strong black coffee and the familiarity
of the actions needed to make it soothed her
shattered nerves a little, but her cottage, usually a
refuge, was suddenly too small to contain her. She
left it to go for a long walk, yearning for company,
for someone she loved to help her, and the solitude
of the footpath did nothing to ease the terrible
empty feeling inside her. She felt hollow, drained
of all feeling and all emotion, and it was just the
shell of a human being that she seemed to have
become that tramped over the fields in a wide
circle around the village.

Hunger and tiredness forced her home in the
end, weary and listless, but she had learned one
thing in her unhappiness. The foul language used
to her and about her did not hurt half so much as
the five simple words at the end of that terrible
letter. 'Something could happen to him.' For
better or worse—and it looked as if it was going to
be for worse—she was falling in love with Luke
Arran, wholeheartedly, singlemindedly and without reservation. It should have made her feel warm
and happy inside, but it did not. She felt afraid
and scorned herself for the emotion. If only the
writer of that letter had waited for one more day,
then it need not have been sent at all. Luke had
already rejected her.

The white Rolls stood before her gate, and she
stopped walking and stared at it in dread. At any
other time she would have been so happy to see it

there, but it was too dangerous now. At the moment she was still shocked enough and weak enough to tell Luke about the letter, and she did not want to do that. Her instinct was to protect him, no matter what the cost.

If she turned round and walked slowly away around the bend in the road, perhaps he wouldn't notice her. If she could get around the bend then she could hide on the footpath that ran under the small stone bridge over the narrow river that skirted the edge of the village. He would not think to look there.

'Kate!' She heard his voice just as she reached the bend, but she refused to run until she was out of sight. Then she climbed down the steep river bank and ducked under the bridge, place of many childhood games when she had been nine or ten years old. She had not come far, but her breath sounded loud in her ears. Would he hear it?

She heard someone running along the road, heard the footsteps falter and then slow down to a walk, and then there was silence. Was he going to give up and go back to the car? It was cold under the bridge away from the heat of the sun and the dampness of the bricks added to the chill so that she shivered suddenly. What was he doing?

'Hi!' Luke appeared down the bank, his height forcing him to stoop a little as he walked under the bridge. 'Is this a private game or can I play too?'

'Luke!' Kate was not in the mood for banter, but she was forced to ask him curiously, 'How did you know I was here?'

'Used to go tracking in the woods with my brothers when I stayed with my grandparents in Oregon.' In the semi-darkness she could see he was grinning. 'You broke a couple of flowers getting down here. Clever, huh?'

'No.' She remembered only too well the circumstances under which they had parted and she resented the lightness of his tone.

'Kate, I'm sorry . . .' His voice deepened and he came closer, seeming very big and very powerful in the confines of the bridge. 'I shot my mouth off this morning. I know it wasn't you. I know you didn't have anything to do with that damned article.'

'Who was it then?'

He shrugged. 'Don't know—yet. I just know it wasn't you.'

'I don't think I want to talk about it.' She made her voice as firm as she could. The threat in that letter now seemed more terrible than ever. 'Go away, Luke.'

'Oh, come on now . . .' He held out a hand, rather as if he was trying to lure a kitten from a small hiding place, but she shook her head and tried to ignore the pleading in his voice. 'Look, I know I've got one hell of a temper—always have had. My ma and pa always say it's the Viking in me. My grandmother was Swedish. Did you know that?'

Kate did not want to hear about his family tree. She just wanted to be left alone. She loved him, and if he talked to her much longer in that soft, gentle voice she would break down and cry.

'It's damp under here,' he continued conversationally, and his fingers scraped at the lichen on the old bricks. 'Can't we talk some place more comfortable? Like your cottage?'

'No, we could not.' Every trace of the letter was gone, but she still felt the stigma of the accusations as though they were written in letters a foot high on her forehead. She turned away from him to walk along the footpath to the bank on the other side of the bridge.

'Katie!' He closed the gap between them so silently that the first indication she had that he was near was when his arms closed around her and she felt warm breath against her ear. 'I'm so sorry, babe. So damn sorry.' His mouth was close to the side of her face. If she turned, just a little, he would kiss her. 'I was a fool not to trust you. I think I went a little crazy this morning.'

Two roads lay before Kate. If she took the easy one she would turn into his arms and let him kiss her. Yet if she did that, she might break down and tell him about the letter, and if he continued to see her then he might be in some kind of danger. It was impossible to judge from the letter how real the threat to him was but, if she refused to see him any more, then he would be safe. That was the hard road.

'Katie ...' She was turned into his arms, unwilling but without the strength to resist him, and his lips touched hers in a light caress of a kiss. '... Katie, I'm sorry ...' and the words were spoken against her mouth so that she inhaled his breath and felt her resolve begin to crumble like the bricks that were a part of the old bridge.

One last kiss. Wasn't she entitled to that? One final chance to put her arms around him and feel his strength and his warmth, one last embrace that would have to comfort her until she could look back at the memories and smile. Even if Luke loved her, and he hadn't said that he did, there were differences in their lives that were irreconcilable. Two people from two different worlds. What chance did they have?

'Am I forgiven?' He was waiting for the words and she had none to give him. She shrugged, a gesture that could have meant anything, but when his lips settled against hers in a long kiss, she could not help herself responding to him, could not help the way her hands tightened on his shoulders or her body pressed itself against his. One last kiss.

The water lapped against the earth bank, somewhere drips of water fell from the roof of the bridge into the river, and in the distance she could hear the bark of a dog, yet nothing was important but this man who held her so securely and so closely. If only she could summon up the courage to tell him what had happened, maybe he would help her. Or maybe he would consider her too much of a liability to his career. She did seem to have brought him nothing but trouble. No, it was better to reject than to run the risk of being rejected. She pulled herself free of his arms.

'I think you'd better go,' she said calmly.

'What?' Luke's forehead creased into a frown of uncertainty.

'I said I think you'd better go.'

'But why? Haven't I explained . . .'

'Yes, you have.' She sought refuge in anger. 'But I don't like being accused of something in my own home, assaulted . . .'

'Assaulted?' He almost shouted the word. 'What the hell do you mean?'

'I mean this . . .' She held out her arm for him to see the dark smudge of bruises around her wrist where he had held her too tightly, and she saw his face set into lines of anger, although she was not sure against whom the anger was directed.

'I'm sorry.' He took her arm before she could withdraw it, and the touch of his fingers was light and caressing against the bruises. 'What can I say to you?' The sapphire eyes were concerned and worried.

'Don't say anything,' she shrugged. 'It isn't important.'

'It is to me.' He raised her arm, bent his head slowly, and she felt the touch of his lips against the inside of her wrist. Light, feathery kisses traced the path of the veins that lay close to the surface, and she shivered. Did he not realise the power he had over her? It was such a simple gesture, but she felt as though she had been running a race and her heart thumped frantically inside her. Could he not hear it? She resisted the urge to touch his wheat-coloured hair and feel the silken strands run through her fingers and wondered why it intrigued her so much.

'Let me go!' She came out of her reverie and snatched her wrist away, facing him squarely. 'You didn't trust me,' she said quietly, 'and I hate that. You hurt me and you made me feel like some kind of gold-digger ...'

'I've said I'm sorry.'

'Yes, but it's not enough. Sorry till the next time?' Wearily she pushed her hair back and shook her head. 'Go away, Luke. Just leave me alone.'

In her flat walking shoes he seemed to tower above her, and for a moment they stared at one another in a brittle silence. Then he shrugged.

'Okay,' he said mildly. 'See you around, babe,' and he turned and left the tunnel.

'Kate, you have got to tell the police.' Clare spoke with a mixture of concern and impatience in her clear voice. 'I can understand your reluctance, but it has to be done.'

'I can't.' Kate, stretched out on a sunlounger with big round sunglasses covering her eyes, spoke in exactly the same quiet tones she had used when she had told her friend about the anonymous letters. She had been forced to. The third one had arrived in the post that day when Clare had been with her. Kate recalled how she had not been able to stop the look of horror that had crossed her face and how she had fled from the room precipitously to shred the awful slip of paper and flush it down the toilet. Clare, of course, had demanded an explanation and, being Clare, had dragged the truth from her. They had returned to Clare's Victorian house outside Toggleton to talk about the subject. Clare had done most of the talking.

'Well, at least tell Luke what's going on. Why should you have to deal with this on your own?' Clare could not hide her exasperation, and Kate tensed, anticipating her next question. 'Is it over between you two?' Clare asked, more gently. 'He doesn't seem to be around any more.'

'I haven't seen him for ten days,' Kate said quietly.

'Yes, but is it over?' Clare asked insistently.

'Yes.' Kate did not elaborate. She saw no need to tell Clare about the letters that arrived every day, delivered by Tony, letters that were loving and funny and full of his optimism that she would want to see him again. 'Well, sort of . . .' she added honestly.

'What does "sort of" mean?'

Kate sighed. 'I haven't seen him, but I've heard from him. We had a . . . a disagreement and I told him to leave me alone, but he's . . . persistent.' It was a good feeling, this warm knowledge that he refused to take no for an answer.

'So tell him!' Clare urged. 'He only lives a couple of miles away. Surely he can spare half an hour of his valuable time. It's all because of him that you're getting the letters.'

'It isn't that simple,' Kate said stubbornly.

'It's exactly that simple.'

Should she tell him? Kate did not know. Several times she had looked at the telephone and wondered if she should call him. Didn't he have a right to know he was being threatened? Even the fact that she was not seeing him had not been enough to stop the letters. And yet . . . and yet she knew that if the threats were to be brought home to him, she would have to tell him something of the rest of the contents of the letters, and this she knew she simply could not do.

Clare was speaking and she had not heard a word she was saying.

'Sorry,' she said, 'I was daydreaming. What did you say?'

'I said,' Clare spoke quietly, 'that you have enough problems and that Luke Arran is just complicating things.'

'What problems?' Kate raised her head and looked over her glasses at Clare's face.

'How long have we been friends?' Clare asked. 'Most of our lives. Yet this is the second time since you've been home that you haven't told me the truth.'

'Oh yes?' Kate asked softly.

'Yes. Once when we went for that walk . . . and now. You've been touchy ever since you came back.'

'I have?'

'You know you have. You're involved . . . more than you'll admit . . . with a man who'll probably hurt you. He already has, indirectly, with that newspaper article. You're getting poison pen letters because of him and you're beginning to look as if you haven't slept for a week. On top of all that, you're not doing any work, although I don't think Luke can be blamed for that. I think you've dried up, run out of words.'

How can she know that, Kate thought frantically? She stared at Clare, sitting cross-legged on the grass clad in shorts and a sun-top, her arms wrapped around her legs, her head tipped slightly on one side as she waited, eyebrows slightly raised, for Kate to answer her.

'Instinct,' Clare said shortly, sensing the unspoken question. 'I know what you're like when you're working on a book. You haven't done anything since you came home.'

'I'm on holiday,' Kate said defensively. She got to her feet and picked up her bag. 'I should be getting back.' Her voice was as casual as she could make it. 'I've got a lot to do.'

Clare stood up too. 'You don't have to go.'

'I think I do.'

Clare looked directly at her friend and Kate knew she could not hide the strain and worry in her face. The big sunglasses hid her eyes, but she knew Clare was too close to her to be deceived by the offhand tone of her voice.

'Don't you think you should stay and talk?' Now Clare's voice was very soft, and Kate felt sudden tears sting her eyes. 'You don't have to do it all on your own.'

Kate hesitated, torn between a sudden urge to sit down and pour out the whole story to her friend, and the knowledge that Clare could do nothing to help her.

'You know you can talk to me,' Clare was saying persuasively, 'and I think you should. If your Luke is too busy . . .' Her voice tailed off as if she realised suddenly that it had been a mistake to mention his name again, and even more of a mistake to mention him in the tone of voice she had used.

'I love him,' Kate said quietly, and seeing the look of exasperation that her friend could not hide, she continued, 'You don't know him. He's kind and gentle and . . .'

'. . . and where is he when you need him?' Clare asked pointedly. 'Why won't you tell him?'

Kate stared at her for a moment, realising suddenly that whatever she said, Clare would not change her opinion of Luke, and suddenly tired of having to defend him to someone who did not even know him. Turning on her heel, blinded by tears, she ran precipitously from the garden, hearing Clare call after her.

CHAPTER SIX

KATE spent the rest of the day in Shersbury,
looking around the antique shops, attending an
auction, and trying to calm herself down. She
knew that at some stage she would have to
apologise to Clare for running out on her and
behaving like a child, but she needed time to
recover herself, and in the anonymity of Shersbury
she found a little peace.

As she drove back to the cottage it was dark
enough to have her headlights on in the gathering
gloom, but she felt stronger now, more able to face
her troubles, and the Imari plate so carefully
wrapped up on the back seat of her car lifted her
spirits a little. It was a long time since she had
treated herself to anything so expensive.

Turning right at the green, her mind still on
some of the beautiful things she had seen but
could not afford, she was shaken out of her reverie
by the array of cars outside her cottage, and the
blaze of lights coming from all the windows.
Apprehensively she eyed the police car standing
outside her gate, and she parked quickly behind
what she recognised as Michael Harroby's Volvo,
while further up the lane she could see the
distinctive shape of Jimmy Bell's old Jaguar.

As she locked the car door, she heard Clare call
her name, and turned to see her friend hurrying
through the gate of the cottage, a cardigan thrown
round her shoulders over her summer dress.

'What's going on?' Kate called sharply, walking

quickly forward to meet her. 'What are the police doing here?'

'Oh, Kate!'

'Hey now!' Alarmed by the distress in Clare's voice, she threw an impulsive arm around her shoulders and hugged her comfortingly. 'What's wrong?'

'It's the cottage.' Kate felt Clare shiver suddenly, despite the cardigan and she saw, in the light of the solitary street lamp, that her friend looked white and shaken. 'No one knew where you were,' Clare continued. 'I . . . we . . . thought something might have happened to you.'

'Happened to me?' Kate echoed. 'Why should anything have happened to me?' Vague suspicions were crowding her mind and making her feel sick. 'What's going on?' she asked again, and now the apprehension was turning to cold fear. Her friend seemed close to tears and just shook her head wordlessly, so Kate released her and walked up the garden path alone, meeting Jimmy and Michael Harroby in the porch.

'My God, am I glad to see you!' Jimmy's voice was unexpectedly shaken and he put his arms around her and hugged her. 'We didn't know what to do!'

'What's wrong?' Jimmy was the calm, unruffled sort. She tried to pull away from him to go into the cottage, but he deliberately blocked her way.

'Kate.' Now Michael claimed her attention, 'Kate, you're in for a bad shock, I'm afraid.'

'You tell her, Mike,' Jimmy urged, and he sounded relieved by the interruption.

'Yes, tell me, Mike,' she agreed, turning to face the tall, quiet doctor and seeing the same expression of strain on his face that she had seen on Jimmy's.

'The cottage has been broken into,' he said quietly. 'As far as we can tell nothing's been stolen, but the place has been ...' he hesitated, then grimaced, '... vandalised.'

'No!' For a moment Kate stood rigid, feeling Jimmy's hands tighten on her shoulders, denying the words that confirmed the suspicion she had been so frightened of. Then she tore herself free and pushed past Michael into the cottage, going straight into the living room that was her safe harbour from the rest of the world.

No. She was not sure if she shouted the word aloud or if she just screamed it inside her head, and for a moment she closed her eyes to deny the evidence of her own sight. Behind her closed eyelids she saw the room as it had been before; serene, comfortable and friendly, but the vision blurred before an onrush of tears, and when she opened her eyes again the havoc swum before her startled gaze.

The room was totally and completely wrecked. A table fork, bent and misshapen, lay on the carpet, and the deep scratches and gouges in the rosewood piano told her what it had been used for. Her dining table and one of her pictures had been attacked in the same way, and her books lay torn and ripped all over the room.

Her upholstery had been slashed, although she could not see any implement lying around that could have caused so much damage, and her chairs and couch and her cream-coloured carpet were splashed with some dark substance which she thought was ink.

She bent to pick up one of her chess pieces, the

white knight, but as she did so the fragment of wood still holding it together snapped and she found herself staring stupidly at the two halves cradled in the palm of her hand. Not the chess set. Please, not the chess set! She got down on her hands and knees and scrabbled around on the floor looking for the other pieces, but the tears were falling now and they hampered her even though she wiped them away with the back of her hand as she searched.

'Kate ...' Jimmy's voice, but she took no notice. She had found the black king and several pawns and the other white knight all undamaged. Maybe there were more, but she mourned the death of the white queen which looked as if someone had tried to grind it into the carpet.

Her father had made this chess set just for her—one of his last gifts. And she and Luke had played the game one warm summer evening. She was good, but he had beaten her. His hands had touched these pieces and she had to find them all.

'Kate!'

Why couldn't they go away and leave her alone? Couldn't they see she was busy?

Something brown caught her eye and she reached under the couch. A china dog, an almost perfect replica of the collie, 'Shadow', that she had grown up with. She had named her new puppy after a dog in an Enid Blyton book and Clare had given her the replica as a birthday present when she was twelve. It was headless.

She raised her head and looked around her. Had nothing in the room been spared? Not one book or one ornament? Fresh tears flowed at the wanton destruction of everything she loved so much.

'Come on, love.' It was Jimmy's voice, close to

her ear. 'There's nothing you can do tonight.' She
felt his hands on her shoulders lifting her up,
turning her from the devastation, and she allowed
him to guide her back to the porch where Michael
and Clare waited, their faces anxious.

Kate looked at them in bewilderment. 'It's
horrible,' she whispered. 'How could anyone do
it?' and she wiped her cheeks with the back of her
hand again.

'I don't know,' Michael said quietly.

'Is every room the same?'

'I'm afraid so. But that room's the worst.'

His voice was grave and she looked from him to
Clare.

'Who could do such a thing?' she asked them, and
gulped as her voice broke. 'Who could do this to
me?' She was beginning to feel sick again and she
still could not really grasp fully what had happened,
unable to take in the enormity of the damage.

'I told the police about the anonymous letters,'
Clare blurted out, and when Kate stared at her
incredulously, she continued quickly, 'I had to—it
might be the same person.'

'Yes.' Kate was too stunned to argue, and when
the local policeman came down the stairs to ask
her questions, she answered woodenly and with
the dazed look still in her face.

What could she tell him? She knew nothing,
suspected nobody, and the letters were all
destroyed.

'Come back with us,' Clare said gently. 'We can
start and clear all this up in the morning.'

She had to make a decision then, and she had to
make it quickly. Part of her wanted to be led away
to the safety of a friendly house where she could
be looked after and comforted. The rest of her—

the part that gritted its teeth and refused to give in—told her to stay. She would admit defeat if she left now and possibly she would never have the courage to come back and live in her home ever again. It was like riding a bicycle, wasn't it? If you fell off you had to get on it again and ride it.

'I'll be fine here,' she said, and smiled unsteadily.

'You can't stay here!' Clearly Michael was surprised. 'It's out of the question. Clare's right— you must come home with us.'

'I'll be all right,' she said stubbornly. 'I won't be frightened into leaving. This is my home and no one's going to scare me away.'

'It isn't a question of courage.' Jimmy Bell still had his arm around her shoulders. 'This place is a mess. Be practical, Kate.'

'I won't go.' Her chin lifted stubbornly.

All three saw the gesture and resigned themselves to losing the argument eventually, although they all tried to get her to change her mind. Jimmy cajoled, Clare pleaded and Michael got impatient with her unreasonable behaviour, but she was quite adamant.

At last they left her alone, and she locked the front door, walked back into the living room and forced herself to try to assess the damage coolly and calculatingly. It was no good. All she could see was the deliberate destruction of the things she loved, and as she walked through into the kitchen and then into the study, where the damage was far less, she realised that whoever was responsible knew just how much her room meant to her.

The implication was frightening. Whoever had done this knew her. It was not just mindless vandalism but vindictive and deliberate damage.

Michael had said outright that she might not be safe here, but she had thought he was just trying to frighten her into leaving. Perhaps he had meant what he said. Perhaps he had realised, as she now realised, that someone hated her.

Methodically she went through the rooms, wincing as she saw the damage done to her electric typewriter, but thankfully realising that her filing cabinet had, for once, been locked, and the key was still in its hiding place.

In the bathroom and the spare bedroom things had just been thrown about casually and there was no real damage, but her own bedroom looked as though it had been hit by a cyclone. Her wardrobe and her chest of drawers had both been emptied and the contents strewn around the room, and all the bedclothes had been pulled off to expose the mattress.

The room reeked of perfume, and as she stepped gingerly over a pile of clothes in the doorway, wrinkling her nose, she saw an empty bottle of her favourite scent lying on top of them. Other bottles, all empty, were arrayed before the dressing table mirror, and with a sinking heart she saw that hand cream and suntan oil had been poured everywhere.

'Oh damn!' she said aloud, and somewhere deep inside her she felt the beginnings of a cold, vengeful fury that she could almost taste. When she had first walked into the room she had wanted to cry, but now the feeling had passed and she only wanted to find the person responsible and ask one question. Why?

Instinctively she guessed that her visitor had been a woman, although she could not have said why. The destruction of her home suggested to her a spitefulness, a vindictiveness, that appalled her, but there was something that was almost childish in the neat line of bottles on her dressing table, something that said, 'Look what I've done!'

Much later, lying in the darkness of the spare room, she moved restlessly in the unfamiliar double bed, listening to every creak and crack of the old cottage settling down for the night, noises that normally she never noticed, but which tonight seemed threatening and strange.

The stairs creaked and she stiffened, her eyes steadfast on the door of her room, watching the handle in frozen fascination. When, after a few minutes, nothing had happened, she relaxed, berating herself angrily for losing her nerve and trying to reassure herself that no one was likely to break in. Despite this she was still afraid, and the fear tempted her to dress and drive over to Clare's house. Only the thought that her appearance would be a tacit acknowledgement that they had been right to want her to leave the cottage kept her in her bed.

Another creak. Her heart lurched and she sat up in the bed, but then her straining ears heard a new noise, the sound of a car coming quietly to a halt outside her cottage, and for a moment she wondered if it could possibly be Luke. Then she realised that it was probably a passing police patrol car keeping an eye on the place, and she hugged her knees with her arms and wished that Luke would somehow, miraculously, arrive on her doorstep.

It would be a miracle too, she thought ruefully. She had ignored his letters and in his one brief telephone call to her, in which he had finally lost his patience and accused her of sulking, she had been frosty. Yet he still hadn't given up.

The knocker was tapped gently and she slipped out of bed and went to the window to see the Rolls, like a white spectre, parked outside. Caught between surprise, relief and then joy, she felt her heart thud heavily and it was several moments before she opened the window quietly and leaned out to call softly, 'Who is it?'

Luke's face, pale in the darkness, turned up to the window.

'Who were you expecting?' he countered. 'Let me in.'

'It's very late.'

'I know that. Open the door.'

'What are you doing here?' Kate asked breathlessly.

'Now there's a damn silly question! Are you going to open up, or am I going to have to start waking the neighbours when I break in?'

'Just a minute.' Flustered by the determination in his voice, she closed the window, pulled on a thin housecoat, and ran barefoot down the stairs.

As soon as she opened the door he pushed past her into the living room and snapped on the light, and she closed the front door, set her back to it, and waited for him in the hall.

'Oh, Kate!' She heard the horror and the anger and the sadness in his voice and bit her lip to stop the weak tears that threatened to choke her.

'Turn the light off,' she said, as steadily as she could. 'I can't look at it again tonight. I can't face it.'

'You were a fool to stay.' His voice was hard as he came back into the hall, but he reached out for her and pulled her close to him, rocking her gently in his arms, and she surrendered to his strength and unspoken sympathy, leaning against him and sliding her arms around his waist. 'I wish I knew what you were trying to prove,' he continued quietly. 'You don't have to show anyone how tough you are—we all know it.'

'I'm not tough,' she protested.

'You're strong and determined and stubborn,' he told her. 'Come back to Pike House with me.'

Back to the wolves, she thought wryly, but she merely said, 'No, thanks, I'm perfectly all right here.'

'Oh yeah? Then why are you shaking?' When she did not reply, Luke said encouragingly, 'Come back with me. You'll be safer there than you are here. I'm frightened that whoever did this might try to hurt you.'

'I've been hurt already.' Hot tears began to slide down her face and she clung to him more tightly. 'Even if I could replace everything, it wouldn't be the same.'

'I know. Poor Kate!'

She broke down completely then, responding to the compassion in his voice, and he held her closely, letting her pour out her heartbreak and her anger in disjointed phrases that made little sense to either of them.

'I'm not tough—I'm not,' she insisted, and then a new thought struck her. 'Who told you about this?' She paused, then raised her head to look at him. 'Clare!'

'She rang me,' Luke admitted. 'She asked me if I'd come over and make you see sense—her words, babe, not mine. She said you shouldn't be alone, but that you were so stubborn she couldn't influence you.' He paused, then added with a hint of admiration in his voice, 'That's some lady. She reminded me of you.'

'She wouldn't like that.' Kate was rapidly becoming calmer under the influence of his practical manner, and the comforting way he was holding her tightly in his arms, protecting her from her own fears.

'Are we going to stand in the hall all night?' Luke asked suddenly.

'It's the only part of the cottage that isn't in chaos.'

'Clare told me it was bad. I thought she was exaggerating, but it seems she wasn't.'

'Look for yourself. The only rooms that aren't too bad are the bathroom and the spare bedroom. I'm sleeping there.' As she spoke Kate became aware of her thin housecoat and the flimsiness of the nightdress beneath it, and her words trailed off nervously.

'All right.' Luke released her abruptly. 'Go and get back into bed. I'll get you some brandy or cocoa or something, then I'll sit on the stairs for the rest of the night.'

'Oh, don't be ridiculous!' Her sense of humour bubbled up at the thought of Luke Arran bringing her cocoa in bed and then sitting on the stairs to guard her. Impulsively she hugged him, tipping her head back so that she could see his face. 'You wouldn't really do that, would you?'

'If I had to.'

Now that she could see him clearly for the first time, there was tiredness and tension etched into every line of his fine-drawn, sensitive face, and, loving him as she did, she could see behind the concern in his eyes to the weariness that he was trying to hide.

'That won't be necessary,' she told him gently, 'and I'll make the cocoa.'

'My idea,' he told her firmly. 'Go to bed, lady.'

'All right.' She did not have the strength to argue with him, and it was a relief to be told what to do. Besides, she had an idea, and she turned and went up the stairs without another word.

When Luke came into the bedroom it was lit only by a small table lamp and, with a mug in each hand, he stared at her in surprise.

'I thought I told you to go to bed.'

'I don't always do what I'm told,' Kate said mildly from her easy chair near the window. 'I'm fine here. You have the bed.'

'Do you really think I'm going to sleep on the bed while you have to sit up all night?' Now he looked cross, and she uncurled herself from the chair and walked up to him in the navy jeans and long-sleeved sweater that she had hastily dressed herself in.

'You look tired,' she said softly, taking the mugs from him and setting them down. 'In fact, you look exhausted. You need the sleep more than I do. I can sleep tomorrow.'

'I'm okay,' he told her.

'And you call me stubborn!' She spoke teasingly, but her hands itched to reach up and touch his face gently, let the fingers trace the lines of strain. 'You sleep,' she told him. 'Please, Luke.'

His face mirrored his indecision and then softened into tenderness. 'You're beautiful,' he said softly, then he was holding her tightly and she was raising her face for his kiss. 'Kate?' His mouth was very close to hers and she felt his breath softly against her skin and waited, not understanding his uncertainty.

'What is it?' she asked.

'Nothing.' He kissed her then, but she sensed

some kind of restraint in him that he had never shown before, and she responded by holding him more tightly, trying to break down his reserve with her hands and her mouth.

His response was immediate, and she gave herself up to him, forgetting all that had happened, her own doubts and fears, in the delight and excitement she felt at being close to him. There was no room for questions, and it was not the time for speech. He was here. His mouth caressed hers and demanded her response, and she became lost and mindless as her instincts to love and be loved took control of her.

The kiss lingered, neither of them wanting it to end, until Luke said suddenly, 'Kate, what are we doing?'

She did not make the mistake of being flippant. 'I'm kissing you,' she said simply, 'and loving every moment of it. What's the matter?'

He sighed and rested the side of his face against the top of her head.

'I want to make love to you.' His voice was only just audible. 'You must know that.'

'Yes.' She guessed what he was going to say next, and swallowed down a feeling of disappointment that was tinged with relief.

'I've made so many mistakes with you,' he told her, and his own face registered his uncertainty, 'and maybe I'm just about to make another one, but I don't think that now is the right time. You're sad and unhappy. I'm sad for you ... and I'd like to kill whoever did this ... It isn't a good way to begin a love affair.' Again he hesitated, and his crystal eyes were very piercing as they locked with her own gaze. 'Or isn't there going to be a love affair?' he asked softly. 'You've got me tied in knots, babe. Our record of trust hasn't been too good, has it? I blamed you for that damn newspaper article and you didn't trust me enough to tell me about those letters.'

'The letters?' Kate spoke the words more sharply than she intended. 'What letters?'

'The ones Clare told me about.'

'Oh, damn her!' And yet she was also relieved. She had not broken her own silent vow to herself that she would not involve him. Having matters taken out of her own hands was something she had not anticipated, although she was sure that Clare would not have done it out of any reason but concern for her. She had said right from the start that Luke should know.

'You should have told me.' He held her loosely within the circle of his arms, and as her forehead crinkled into a frown, he leaned forward and kissed it lightly.

'Maybe,' she admitted unwillingly, 'but I couldn't. You'd have wanted to know what was in them, and I couldn't have told you. I didn't even tell Clare. They were ...' she wrinkled her nose, '... disgusting!'

'I love it when you do that.' This time the kiss was planted between her eyes. 'Did you think I'd be shocked?' He was going to persist until he got an answer; she knew him well enough to understand that.

'I thought maybe you might believe some of it,' she admitted. 'And I didn't think I knew you well enough to be able to judge how you'd react. You might have thought I was involving you too much.' She shrugged. 'I don't know.'

'Oh, Kate, Kate ...' Luke pushed her hair away from her forehead again and then pulled her close.

'You're dumb, did you know that?' His lips teased her ear and she shivered. 'I'm glad Clare told me. I'd have been even more glad if you'd called me yourself. I do wish you weren't so damn independent. I wish you'd trust me.'

'I didn't want to worry you.' She cringed inwardly from the feeble excuse. She prided herself on her honesty. Why couldn't she be honest with him? Because it might hurt him?

'Worry me?' he echoed, and abruptly he released her to walk over to the window and stand with his back to her, staring out over the green. 'Don't you know I'd do anything for you? You're not stupid. Can't you see I'd have been . . . over the moon . . . if you'd called me and told me you needed me?'

'I'm sorry.' She had hurt him, and she eyed his broad back and the weary droop of his shoulders with a mixture of uncertainty and concern. 'I did think about ringing you—I really did.'

'What went wrong, then?' He swung round to face her. 'Wouldn't your pride let you admit that for once you needed someone to help you?'

'That's not fair!' She was stung by the bitterness in his voice.

'Isn't it? You had people like Clare and Jimmy Bell who all wanted to help you tonight, but you wouldn't let them. It isn't weak to accept help, you know, and at least it would show everyone that you're still human.' Luke hesitated, then said firmly; 'If you hadn't met me then you wouldn't have got the anonymous letters and your home wouldn't be in the state it's in tonight. I don't know who's doing this to you, but I'll find out if it takes me the rest of my life. That beautiful room . . .' His voice tailed off and he shook his head.

'I'm sorry you had to see it like that,' Kate said quietly. 'I know you loved it.'

Silence. Luke stared at her expressionlessly, and although the actual distance between them was only a few feet, she felt suddenly that there was miles and miles of empty space separating them, and that nothing she could say would breach the gap.

'I came to see you,' he said quietly, 'not the damn room.'

'All right, all right!' She was too tired and too depressed to watch her words and she snapped at him. 'Why should you think I'd call you anyway?' she said crossly. 'We aren't on the best of terms.' And the memory of their last meeting rose up in her mind to shame her.

'Maybe because I was fool enough to think there was still something between us.' There was an edge of anger in his voice too. 'I thought you were playing some kind of game ... should have known better ... but then I've never met anyone like you before.'

The room was suddenly too small to contain them both. Kate did not want to fight him, was too tired to fight him, and her weariness was making her lose control of her tongue. If it went much further she would tell him that she loved him—irrevocably and passionately—and to speak of love with the tension still between them would be fatal.

'Okay ...' he seemed to sense her exhaustion, 'there's no point in going on with this. Not tonight. Maybe it'll all seem better in the morning.' He came back towards her and grasped her hand, lifting it to study the wrist that he had hurt. 'The bruises are almost gone,' he said. 'I'm glad about that.'

He looked up at her and his face was very close, so close that she could see the laughter lines around his eyes and the smallest of scars at the side of his nose. The soft glow of the lamp highlighted the planes of his face and Kate wondered if it was her imagination or the lighting that made it seem thinner than ever.

'We're going to talk tomorrow,' he warned her. 'I've got a lot to say and you're going to listen. Then you can tell me how you feel and maybe we'll get a little truth between us at last.'

'If that's what you want.' She was bowing to his demands and surprising herself with the meekness of her voice.

'That's exactly what I want.' Luke smiled, and the lines around his eyes deepened. 'Now drink your cocoa like a good girl and let's share this bed.'

'Oh no!' On this point at least she would not yield. 'I'll never sleep anyway. I'll just toss and turn and disturb you.'

'Okay.' He sighed, suddenly seeming too tired to argue with her any further, and then, by unspoken agreement, they parted; she to her chair with her mug while Luke sat on the side of the bed and gulped down his drink. When he had finished she switched out the light and, as he pulled off his shoes and lay down, she covered him with a light blanket that she had put ready at the bottom of the bed.

She enjoyed being able to do something for him, liked the feeling that she was looking after him, and she lingered over the simple task, twitching the blanket until it covered him completely. As she wished him goodnight and turned away, he caught

hold of her arm and made her turn back towards
him.

'You know something?' His voice was slurred
with sleep. 'You're a bully!'

'Thank you, kind sir.'

'Kiss me?' She stooped over him, and he
accepted the touch of her lips and closed his eyes
tiredly.

'Sleep well,' she told him.

Back in her own chair she relaxed and burrowed
into the blanket she had brought from her own
bedroom. For a few minutes there was silence,
then Luke's voice came plaintively from the bed in
the dark silence of the room,

'This is ridiculous,' he said. 'Come and sleep
with me.'

'I'm comfortable here,' she told him. 'Hush!'

A heavy sigh answered her and she grinned in
the darkness, but after that there was peace, and in
the quietness she turned her mind back to their
conversation.

She loved him, and she had almost told him so
in a weak moment. It was difficult to think
objectively about that love when she was so tired,
but she made herself look on Luke Arran as just a
person whose way of life was alien to hers. She
knew little of singers or actors or the profession to
which they belonged, but what she had read
suggested to her a superficiality and a lack of
permanence that was disquieting.

What would the word love mean to a man like
him? Did he tell all his women he loved them? He
hadn't told her yet. Was love to him a
commitment, or just a word he used as he flitted
from pretty girl to pretty girl? Did he realise that if
she ever talked about love, she would mean a deep

and lasting emotion? Would he understand how
much he could hurt her?

She had loved a man once before, and briefly
she remembered dark-haired, elegant Miles, wondering at how quickly her love for him had died.
At the time she had thought she was going to cry
for the rest of her life, and nothing had meant
anything to her. She had travelled, and looked at
the world with eyes that saw nothing, meeting
people and not being able to remember their
names or their faces ten minutes later. Would she
have to go through that again because she loved
Luke?

She opened her eyes and strained them to look
at the man lying on the bed. She guessed that he
was asleep already, and she wondered what it
would be like to be in the bed with him.

The thought made her move restlessly in the
chair which had seemed so comfortable at first,
but which was now suddenly hard and unyielding.
So many questions, and none that she could
answer because he held the key. Only one nagged
at her until she wriggled again in her chair and
longed for the peace of sleep. What basis for love
did they have?

Their knowledge of one another was limited to a
few short conversations in her living room, a walk
on the beach and this evening's brief closeness.
They had no shared experiences or friends, and the
roots of their friendship were fragile and slender.
She had only seen one side of him, as he had only
seen one side of her. She had never seen him at
work, and he had never seen her when she was
writing. They had always been on their guard
when they had met.

They had a few things in common, she could

admit that, but a love of music and books seemed
so very little. Her thoughts rambled on as she grew
sleepy and her head grew too heavy for her neck to
support it. She felt it droop, was too tired to stop
it and too weary even to raise it, when she heard a
rustle from the bed. Luke must be turning over in
his sleep.

She was surprised but not alarmed when she felt
herself lifted, still wrapped inside her blanket, and
carried bodily over to the bed. The linen of the
pillow was cool and comforting against her cheek
and she snuggled blissfully into the softness, a little
smile twitching around her lips as she felt Luke
tuck the blanket more snugly around her shoulders
in the same way as she had done for him. The bed
dipped as he got in on the other side, then he was
drawing her close and dropping a light kiss on her
nose.

'You didn't really think I'd let you do it, did
you?' His voice was soft and mocking. 'You really
don't know me very well, do you?'

No, perhaps she didn't. She let her smile widen a
little, but the effort to talk was too much. She let
herself drift away into sleep.

CHAPTER SEVEN

IT was the sun that woke her, streaming brightly and relentlessly through a gap in the curtains directly onto her face. She turned her head away from it and slitted one eye open to look at the clock on the small table that stood at the side of her bed. Only she couldn't see it. All she could see was the tumbled blond hair of the man who lay fast asleep beside her, face relaxed and oddly vulnerable in slumber, clear blue eyes hidden from her, mouth slightly parted to show his even white teeth.

Luke. Luke? Forcing her sleepy brain to recall the events of the previous night, Kate could just remember being put into the bed next to him and not having the strength to protest. Or not wanting to protest.

He really did have a superb face. If she was an artist, she would be itching to capture the fine-boned features on canvas. She was so close to him that she could see the faint beading of sweat on his upper lip and the dampness of the hair that fell over his forehead. She propped herself up on to one elbow and gave herself up into rapt contemplation of his features.

Even in sleep his face was strong, the jaw as determined as her own, but it was his mouth that drew her attention and made her remember the way he had kissed her the previous night. It had a quality of sensuousness about it, as if this man knew all about love, but even in sleep he looked as

110

if he was going to smile at any moment, and she
liked that above everything else.

'Morning.' The word was a mumble of sound,
but it startled her. Then she saw the blue of his
eyes through his long, fair eyelashes and knew that
he had been watching her.

'Good morning.' This was a situation she was
not sure of, and she cursed the tremor in her voice.

Luke rolled on to his back and stretched until
his muscles cracked, yawning widely and then
rubbing his hand over his face, while Kate
watched him in silent fascination. Then he pulled
her down to lie beside him, and she fought against
pushing away and meekly allowed him to pillow
her head comfortingly against his shoulder.

'How do you feel?' he asked quietly.

'Fine. Not looking forward to going downstairs,
though.'

'I'll be with you. Don't worry.'

'Mmm.' She still wasn't fully awake, and
drowsily she watched the curtains flutter at the
half open window and heard the distant sound of
the dogs barking up at the kennels just outside the
village. Familiar sounds, sounds that she heard
every morning. Only this morning was different.
She lay in an unfamiliar bed with Luke Arran's
arms wrapped around her, and she was happy and
contented.

'Are you still glad I came last night?'

'Yes.'

'Do you know why I came?'

That was a question that was difficult to answer.
She could hope, but she did not know for sure.
What was she supposed to say?

'Tell me.' Gently she threw the onus back on
him to make his feelings clear, and she rubbed her

cheek against the soft cotton shirt that he was still wearing in a small gesture of encouragement.

'For the same reason I kept writing you letters. For the same reason that I realised you couldn't have written that article ... and I wouldn't have cared if you had ... for the same reason that made me so angry that you hadn't told me about those damn letters.'

'What reason was that?' But there could only be one explanation, and a bubble of happiness was growing inside her slowly so that she wanted to shout aloud her joy.

'You want me to spell it out?' Luke laughed softly. 'Three words, Katie, the three most important words in the world. I love you.' Yes, it had to be that, and the bubble inside her expanded until she thought she would suffocate with the sensation. 'Hey ...' his fingers underneath her jaw turned her face up to his, '... did you hear me?'

'Oh, Luke ...' She had so much more than love to give him. She wanted to be his friend, his companion, his sanctuary when he was tired.

'I know it's early in the morning, my love,' his mouth was smiling at her, but his eyes held a hint of wariness, 'but couldn't you manage a few more words? Or have I said the wrong thing again?'

'I love you.' She said the three words slowly as she held his gaze, and tried to make them into a declaration of faith. 'I love you so much. But, Luke ...'

'No!' His expression changed suddenly and became determined. 'Not now. Isn't it just enough to know how we feel?'

It was, and when his arms went tightly around her, she raised her face for his kiss, taking as her right the passionate lips that moved on hers, the hands that stroked her back, the long hard body that she was pressed against, and in return giving all she was in that breathless, incredible moment when the bubble inside her burst and the love that she had for him could be expressed. Her mouth opened beneath his like a flower seeking the sun and she felt herself pressed into the bed as his body moved over hers, accepting the weight gladly and feeling herself covered and protected by his strength.

'Kate.' His mouth moved along her jaw and down to her throat, and she relaxed under the caresses and felt her whole body singing like a guitar that had been softly strummed and the echoes of its chord left to hum in the silence. She had found what she had been looking for and her world was contained within her arms.

'I've never been so happy!' Luke flung himself away from her suddenly and pillowed his head in his hands as he lay on his back and stared at the ceiling. 'This is the first day of the rest of our lives. Did you know that?'

His sudden movement away from her had left Kate feeling oddly stranded. A moment ago they had been one passionate, exciting unit, crushed together and showing their love openly and without reserve, and now Luke had distanced himself from her deliberately without telling her why. Then she understood.

'Hey . . . you!' She followed him across the bed, closing the gap between them, and she leaned over him and smiled down into his face. 'What are you doing over here?'

'Oh . . .' his voice was a mixture of frustration and amusement, 'you know damn well. It's nine o'clock in the morning and any minute now some of your ever-loving friends will be round to help sort out that mess downstairs.'

'So?' Mischievously she teased him, laughing aloud as his frustration became more pronounced.

'So I'd like to spend all day in bed making love to you ... but I can't. Half the village will be round soon, and I think they might distract us.'

'Who cares?' She was so secure in her love, so confident of the future, that she was prepared to be reckless.

'I care.' He raised his head and kissed each corner of her laughing mouth gently. 'I want it to be right. Moonlight, candles, flowers ... everything.'

'You're a romantic!' Kate just could not stop smiling, could not resist bending her head and kissing each of the eyebrows that quirked upwards in matching amusement.

'So sue me,' he murmured. 'Wouldn't you like it to be like that too? We can afford to wait, can't we?' And then, with a sudden surge of forceful words, 'Don't smile at me like that, damn you! Don't you know what you do to me? Come here ...'

She was pulled against him, the breath knocked from her body, and then his mouth found hers and kissed her, causing a wild tingle through her body and turning her blood to liquid flame. Was it like that for him too? Did he feel the same sweet desire that she did, did he want to know and understand everything about her as she wanted to know everything about him? Her body seemed light, supple and pliant and yielding to his male strength, and the hungry mouth that covered her neck and throat increased the sharp, thrilling excitement within her.

'Oh, Luke!' She did not care about flowers and moonlight. All that she wanted was in this bed with her; all that she would ever need was this man who had her wrapped tightly in his arms and was whispering endearments to her in a voice that shook.

The letterbox rattled.

Kate froze, remembering instantly how she had come to dread that sound in recent days. Not another letter! Not now, when heaven was so close. She had to get to it before Luke did, had to destroy it before he—in his buoyant happiness— could demand to share it with her. Wouldn't she share anything with him, give him anything? Yes, anything but this sordid stain on their new love.

She pushed herself free, and he seemed so surprised by her action that he released her.

'Back in a minute.' She fled from the room, not daring to look at him, and pattered quickly down the stairs to see that plain white envelope on the mat. Oh no—not again! Not today, of all days, when she just wanted to be happy. She would burn it without opening it. She would not allow it to hurt her.

'Another letter?' She glanced up the stairs in panic and saw Luke standing there, his eyes on the envelope in her hand.

'No.' How could she do anything but lie to him?

'Yes, it is, love. I can tell from your face. Let me see . . .' Slowly he came down the steep staircase, hand outstretched, and when Kate made an involuntary gesture to run, he took the last four in a single jump and landed precisely in front of her. 'Let me see,' he said again.

'Luke, please! I wasn't going to read it—I just want to burn it. Please!'

Another test of trust for them when their love was perhaps too fragile to bear it. She wanted him to trust her enough to let her burn it without opening it, and she could tell from his face that he wanted her to let him read it, and to trust him not to be affected by its contents.

'I have to know.' There was a determination in his face that she had never seen before. She hardly recognised the stern set of his jaw or the way his eyebrows drew together in a frown. 'Kate, please. I have to know.'

And once he knew—what then? Rejection? Or would their love be strengthened by his belief in her, and conversely by her reliance on the depth of his feelings.

'All right.' It went against all her inner convictions that she should deal with this by herself, that she had to have the strength to ignore the letters that wanted to hurt her, but it was a relief to be weak and to hand it over with fingers that trembled.

He noticed the tremor and his face softened miraculously. Gently, deliberately, he lifted her hand and kissed each finger individually, and then he took her letter and walked into the kitchen, his feet crunching over a packet of spilled breakfast cereal that he obviously did not notice in his preoccupation.

She could not bear to watch him while he opened it and read the infamous words that it would contain, and could hardly endure the speculation of wondering exactly what she had been accused of this time. She sat on the stairs, elbows propped on her knees and her chin cupped in her hands, staring abstractedly at the front door and listening to the silence. Absentmindedly she realised that there were fingermarks on the white paint next to the light switch and made a mental note to clean them off.

A match was scraped against its box in the kitchen. Kate guessed that he had read the letter and was destroying it. What would he look like when he came back into the hall?

When he scuffed his way back through the cornflakes his face was pale beneath its Californian tan and his mouth was a thin, straight, angry line. An anger that was bitter but controlled. Anger against whom?

'You're stupid!' He came and knelt in front of her as she sat on the stairs, and his fingers twined themselves into her hair and tugged gently. 'Stupid and dumb and ridiculously independent.'

'Thanks!'

'You're very welcome.' Luke tried to smile, but the terrible tension was still there and she waited for the outburst. 'I can understand why you didn't want to show me.' He ducked his head so that the sapphire eyes were hidden from her. 'It was a filthy, obscene letter. Whoever wrote it must have a mind like a sewer.' His voice hardened and became edged with fury. 'The police should have stopped it getting through!'

'They told me not to burn any more,' Kate confessed.

'I wouldn't allow you to show it to them!' Suddenly his head came up proudly and arrogantly. 'I love you.' His voice held all the confidence in the world. 'If any more come then we'll burn them together without opening them. But I'm going to be here with you. And I'll find out who's doing it.'

'Luke . . .'

'What, love?'

Kate disentangled his fingers from her hair and held them tightly in her lap.

'I don't know what that letter said, but . . .'

'. . . but it isn't true.' Luke finished the words for her and suddenly his hands twisted in hers so that he was holding her fingers. 'Of course it isn't true, damn you! Did you think I'd believe one single word? What do you think I am? God, you're even dumber than I thought you were!'

'I'm scared of losing you.' She could tell him the truth now, but the letters remained like a scar across their love. Nothing would be completely right until they had stopped.

'I love you.' He repeated his earlier declaration. 'If you can find some way for me to prove it to you, then I will. Jump through fire? Fight a duel? Whatever.'

'Just find out who wrote those letters.'

'Do you know?' He stood up and she made room for him to sit beside her on the stairs. Tightly squeezed against him, she still did not have the confidence to voice her suspicions.

'No,' she said quietly.

'I think you have an idea.' Could he really read her so easily? As she turned to look at him, those expressive eyes had narrowed and were speculative as they stared at her. 'Just like I have.'

'A woman, maybe?' she hazarded. 'They say it's a woman's weapon, don't they?'

'So far we agree.'

'I don't know any more than that. But then I didn't know anyone hated me that much.'

'Do you think it's someone connected with me rather than someone you know?'

'Maybe,' she shrugged.

'You aren't being very helpful. Are you trying to protect me or something?'

'Would I need to?' she countered softly, reaching out for his hand and squeezing his fingers.

'No.' Luke continued to frown over the problem. 'Do you think it could be one of the film crew? Is that why you aren't talking? I know you haven't met them, but they do know about you.'

'Honestly, Luke, I don't know.' Kate did not dare to suggest that he looked more closely at his immediate circle of friends. Friends like Sandy and Nancy. 'Two of the letters have threatened you though. Oh,' she qualified the statement quickly, 'nothing specific. But you must be careful.'

'If I stay here with you, then we can look after one another.' The sun came out with his smile. 'Would you like that?'

'Yes.' And with the soft affirmative she felt as though some kind of commitment had been made between them.

'Okay. Let's get dressed then we can talk some more.' He got to his feet and pulled her up. 'Well,' he temporised, 'I guess we're dressed already, aren't we? You comb your hair and I'll brew some coffee. If there's any left.'

'Yes, sir!' As she turned to go, he caught hold of her and pulled her hard against him.

'You want some help?' His voice veered between amusement and an attempt at a lecherous leer.

'No, thank you.' She reached up to kiss him swiftly and then ran up the stairs lightly to hear his laughter ring around the hall.

The jeans and sweater in which she had spent the night were crumpled and she wanted to change, but was there anything left for her to wear that was not stained or torn? The wrecked bedroom sobered her swiftly, but the sun was streaming in through the window and Luke was clattering around downstairs, and Kate forced her swift feeling of depression into the background as she picked over the dresses and trousers and tried to be objective about the chore.

When she finally returned downstairs, clad in brown cord dungarees with a bib and straps over a white sweater, and high-heeled flimsy sandals, Luke had found a big sack and was throwing away all the packages and broken jars that lay on the floor. The coffee was bubbling happily. He glanced up as she walked into the kitchen and whistled.

'Lady, you look fantastic!'

'Thank you, kind sir.'

'You look about sixteen . . . do you know that?' He came over to her, wrapped his arms around her waist and lifted her bodily off the ground. 'Innocent and sexy and beautiful. My sweet Kate!'

She rubbed her face against his. 'You're prickly,' she commented. 'Are you going to go back to change or something?'

'Nope. Brought a razor and stuff in the car.'

'Oh? You came well prepared, then?' She teased him with the words, feeling the earlier mood of euphoria return. He could do that to her. He could make her feel happy and lighthearted, banishing the depression as though it had never existed.

'I'm always well prepared.' He put her down and walked to the kitchen door. 'I don't eat breakfast,' he said. 'Do you?'

'Not usually. Just coffee.'

'How nice to be able to agree on something at last!' and then he was gone and Kate heard him

whistling as he went out through the front door to
go to the car. The whistling continued as he ran
upstairs, but then a plaintive voice floated down to
her:

'Forgot my toothbrush. Can I borrow yours?'

'I thought you were always well prepared!' she
called back.

'So I was wrong!'

'Just don't tell my dentist.'

'Lady, I love you!'

Kate shook her head and smiled, pouring the
coffee into two large mugs and marvelling at the
feeling of intimacy that they had managed to
create between them in the small cottage. The
sheer domesticity of making coffee for him, the
fact that he was singing to himself in the
bathroom, the idea of them sharing a toothbrush,
all increased her feeling of happiness, and she
walked into the living room and used her new and
shining love as a shield against the horror of what
lay before her. With Luke beside her, she knew she
could face anything. Sighing, she sat on the floor
and began to sort her books.

CHAPTER EIGHT

'I THOUGHT they'd never go!' Luke flung himself down on to the couch and hooked his long jean-clad legs over the side.

'It's been quite a day,' Kate agreed, carrying the last of the tea-cups into the kitchen and then returning to the living room to watch him affectionately. So many people had called on them, offering help and sympathy, that the hours had been full and tiring.

Clare had been round and so had Jimmy, and the pair of them had stayed for most of the day. Miss Mole had arrived to dispense tea and sympathy and chocolate cake and had also remained to help clean up one of the bedrooms.

More surprisingly, Ray Robbins and Tony Royal had turned up on her doorstep, and she was sure that their concern and anger had been genuine. So had their willingness to work, and she had been surprised by their practicality. Ray had spent most of the day repainting stained walls—a job he had confessed with a grin to enjoying—and Tony had gone back to Pike House and returned with rugs to cover the worst of the marks on her carpet and groceries to fill her empty shelves.

Despite the depressing nature of their work, eveyone had seemed determined to be cheerful, and Kate had been swept along by their optimism, but it was Ray's quiet words that had done more to help her than anything.

'I want you to know I'm sorry about the party,'

he had said quietly when they were alone for a few minutes. 'Yes, I was interfering, and Luke's had a few words to say on the subject, but I won't do it any more. I saw Luke's face last night when that friend of yours rang. He'd have to be serious about you to look like that.'

Kate had raised an eyebrow, not knowing quite what to say.

'I'm not your enemy,' he had assured her. 'I've never seen Luke this way about a lady before. Neither has Tony.'

'What way?' she had queried the words.

'Protective. Fierce. I don't know . . . different.'

Different? In love? Was that what he had meant? She did not know.

'Come over here.' Luke held out his hand to her and she crossed the room and curled up on a rug at his feet. 'How do you feel now?'

'Happier now that everything's tidied up. Ray and Tony were a great help.'

'Good. Guess the place looks a little bare, though.'

It did. Kate glanced around the room and sighed at the emptiness of the walls. The table and piano had been considerably covered with bright cloths by Miss Mole to try and hide the deep scratches, and the rugs on the floor hid the worst of the stains, but the most pitiful sight to her was the few remaining chessmen who were arrayed on the mantel of her fireplace in a pathetic line.

'Can't replace those, love.' Luke saw the way her eyes were looking. 'I could go out tomorrow and buy you a new chess set, but it wouldn't be the same. Hey . . .' there was a sudden eagerness in his voice, 'would you like me to? I'd like to buy you something. How about a chess set?'

'Thank you.' She was touched by his under-standing. 'I'd love that.'

'Good!'

He had an infectious impetuosity, this nearly-lover of hers. He had worked harder than anyone that day, but whenever she had looked at him or gone close to him, his eyes had always been on her and a little smile had always lurked around his mouth. As if they shared a secret. Which they did.

'Clare brought over a chicken casserole and a lemon meringue pie,' she told him. 'At least we won't starve. What time do you want to eat?'

'I'd better go home and change first.' Luke indicated his casual clothes. 'I'm not dressed for candlelight dinners.'

'Must you?' She did not want him to go back to Pike House. Whoever was sending her the letters would know where he had spent his day.

'Don't you want to be on your own?' The hand that was holding hers squeezed gently. 'I'm sorry, I didn't think . . .' He paused, frowned, then seemed to reach a decision. 'I'll call Tony, have him bring me some clothes down here. Okay?'

'Yes.' She was much happier with the idea that she would not have to be without him, even for a short while.

'You know something?' Luke tipped his head back and stared at the oak beam above his head. 'I feel more at home here than I do in my own place.'

'Where do you live exactly?' asked Kate.

He shrugged. 'Los Angeles. I've got a small place by the beach. It's pretty there, but I'm not around too often.'

'What,' she could not resist mocking him, 'no swimming pool? No sauna?'

'Nope. But it's got the most incredible view of the ocean. You'd love it. It's quiet and peaceful and beautiful.'

'I'm sure I should.' Deliberately she changed the subject, not certain that she wanted to discuss whether or not she would like his home. 'How about a stroll before we have dinner?'

'Aren't you tired?'

'Yes, but I'd like a breath of air. We only need go a little way.'

'Okay.'

Luke got to his feet and they went out to walk hand in hand up as far as Jimmy's garage and then across the fields in a small semi-circle around the back of the village to the cottage again.

In that short time Kate learned more about him—about his interest in conservation, and his love for the beauty and the wildness of nature. With him she admired the intricate shaping of a leaf and, with her head close to his, watched a ladybird crawl along the back of his hand. Then she sat and made a daisy chain in lazy idleness while Luke climbed the short, steep hill that would give him a view of three counties.

He seemed to have unlimited energy, but the open air was reviving her too, that and the feeling of anticipation that was building slowly and sweetly between them. It had been there all day, feeding on the secret love that they shared and on the knowledge that neither of them would have to be alone that night.

Nancy would be alone. Kate sat up straight and stared at the figure of Luke as he stood at the top of the hill, king of all he surveyed. She had never told him about the small scene in his bedroom and did not want to, but the more she thought about

it, the more her instincts told her that it was
Nancy who was behind all her troubles. Or was
that too obvious? She didn't want to think about
it. The evening ahead of her had to be perfect and
she did not want anything to spoil it. When they
got home she wanted to lock the door on the rest
of the world and re-create that very special
atmosphere of intimacy that they had shared
before.

The daisy chain was finished. When Luke came
down the hill again she hung it around his neck as
a token of thanks, she said, for all that he had
done, and then could not persuade him to take it
off again. They finished their walk with the
garland still slung around his shoulders while he
recounted a trip to Hawaii and the festoons of lei
that had been presented to him. 'I'd rather,' he
said gently, 'have this.'

At the cottage, by unspoken agreement, they
retired to separate bedrooms to change, making a
small ceremony out of the act that sent a tingle of
anticipation down Kate's backbone at the look of
promise in Luke's eyes.

Was this what it would be like if they were
together for the rest of their lives? Would she
always need him and want him as much as she did
now? Would there always be the same sense of fun
between them as she slipped into the bathroom
ahead of him and then sang in the shower for the
sheer joy of being alive, forgetting that he was a
professional singer with many years of experience
behind him?

'Kate?' He rapped sharply on the bathroom
door.

'Won't be long,' she called back.

'It isn't that. Do you have to sing so loudly?'

'Why?'

'Darling, I love you ... but you don't sing in tune.'

'Go away!'

The shower was invigorating, and as she looped a huge bath sheet around her shoulders and used one corner of it to wipe the condensation off the small mirror in the room, her face looked back at her and she smiled at her own reflection. Gone was the wary expression that seemed to have become a part of her face in recent weeks, and now her lips curved lightheartedly and her forehead was smooth and unruffled.

'You're vain,' she told herself severely, but the face in the mirror continued to smile, and she shook her head and slipped back into her own room to dress, blessing Clare for her thoughtfulness in bringing over one of her own dresses for Kate to borrow.

Memories of their younger days when they had doubled their wardrobes by borrowing one another's clothes slipped through her mind as she dressed swiftly, knowing that the dress would fit her perfectly but still eyeing herself critically in the mirror as she put her make-up on. Green was a colour that she wore very seldom, but she liked the simplicity of the style and the way the material hung and guessed that Clare had probably lent her the newest and most expensive dress in her wardrobe. Bless her! She would have to find some way to pay her back.

She grinned as she remembered the look of trepidation that Clare had given her when she had first arrived that morning. She had obviously been unsure of her welcome after her unsolicited assistance of the night before. Kate had just smiled sunnily at her and Clare had grinned back in obvious relief, asking quietly later on and when they were alone if she had done the right thing. Kate had just looked and nodded, and Clare had blown out her cheeks in an exaggerated sigh of relief.

Luke was still dressing when she slipped downstairs, checked the casserole in the oven and shook her head over her forgetfulness in omitting to uncork the wine before she went upstairs. They had laid the table between them, covering the ugly scars on its satiny surface with a lacy cloth, and she lit the candles and surveyed the room critically, sighing as its plainness caught at her heart again. She had hung the new Imari plate, but it was only replacing two that were now smashed, the pieces carefully put into a box to see if they could be repaired.

'Hi!' Two long arms snaked around her waist and a hard jaw rested against her shoulder. She started slightly and then relaxed into the embrace, leaning back against him and turning her face so that she could rub her cheek against his. 'I've got something for you.' He loosened one of his arms enough to wave a small box in front of her nose. 'I bought it a while ago, but I haven't had the nerve to give it to you before now—thought you might throw it at me.'

'Oh, Luke!'

'Oh, Luke!' He mimicked her outraged tone perfectly. 'Well, you are a very formidable lady, you know. You want to see what it is?'

Pleased by his thoughtfulness, intrigued by the small square package, Kate unwrapped the shiny red paper and opened the box it concealed. The thick silver bracelet was exquisite in its simplicity and hung heavily from her fingers as she examined it.

'It's beautiful!' She put it on her wrist and admired it.

'I've noticed you don't wear much of that kind of thing,' he told her, 'just your ring. So I didn't think you'd like anything ... well ... fancy.' He was quite right, and she was touched by the fact that he had considered her taste before making his purchase. 'And I bought it myself.' He turned her to face him and linked his arms around her waist again in a loose embrace. 'Even wrapped it myself. Not like those flowers I sent you after the accident.'

'Oh, love!' That revelation gave her so much pleasure—not so much the fact that he had gone into the shop himself, but that he had realised it was important for her to know. 'Thank you.'

'Do I get a kiss?' There was a smile on his face, but the question was almost shy.

'I love you!' She hugged him tightly for a moment and then leaned forward to brush her lips against his. When she drew back, he raised an eyebrow at her.

'Is that the best you can do?' he asked ruefully.

Her turn to tease him a little. 'For now,' she told him demurely. 'Dinner's ready.'

'Dinner can wait.' One arm locked around her until she could hardly breathe, and his other hand tangled itself into her hair. 'I've got one question,' he continued. 'What was Jimmy Bell playing at this morning? I mean, it seemed as though he knew you pretty well. Have I got competition? I didn't know that you and he ...' His voice trailed off but his eyes questioned hers.

'Jimmy's a good friend,' she told him. 'He did

ask me to marry him a while ago, but I said no—I don't love him that way. He was asking me about you this morning.'

'What did you tell him?'

'Nothing. But I think he's guessed. He's always like that.' She saw she was going to have to explain Jimmy Bell a little more. 'I've known him since we were children,' she told him. 'It doesn't mean anything.'

'I hope not!' The arm around her tightened a little more. 'I was jealous. I wanted to kick them all out and have you to myself. I think you're going to have a possessive lover, Katie.'

Lover. For a second she wondered bleakly if that was all she would ever be to him, but the feeling of wariness passed as he bent and took her lips in a kiss that cherished her mouth and gave only a hint of the desire he had shown earlier. It was a sweet kiss that promised all but was still light and tender, and she responded helplessly to the wonder of the moment and the presence of the man who was holding her.

Later, after they had eaten and Luke had helped her to clear away the dishes, showing an eagerness to share the domestic chores that made her smile, she switched on the music centre, which had not suffered too badly, and he sat on the couch, stretching his long legs out in front of him.

'I don't have any of your records,' she said apologetically, looking at him over her shoulder as she lowered the lid. 'Sorry.'

'You don't like my voice?' The question was asked plaintively, but she saw the amusement in his eyes.

'Of course I do,' she said soothingly, 'I just prefer classical music.'

'I'll forgive you.' He stretched his arms above his head and she walked over to the settee and sat beside him. Immediately his arm came down to encircle her shoulders and draw her close.

'What shall we do tomorrow?' he asked.

'We could go to the beach.' Kate rested her head against his shoulder and sighed happily. 'Or we could go to the moor. I don't mind.'

'Shall we go to London and get your chess set?'

So he hadn't forgotten. She smiled and shook her head.

'I don't think we'll need to. Shersbury's just the sort of place where we'll find one.'

'Whatever you want.' He paused and then she heard the hesitation in his voice. 'I've got a confession to make, Kate.'

'What?' She was amused rather than anxious. He sounded like a guilty schoolboy.

'I have to fly back to the States in four days.'

'What?' She had not expected that. Yet had not Ray said earlier in the day that Luke's part in the filming was over? Maybe she should have expected something of the kind. 'Do you have to?'

'I'm not happy about it,' he admitted, 'but I don't have a lot of choice. But does it need to make any difference to us? Come back with me.'

'To the States?' she asked blankly, stupidly.

'Yes.'

What as? Prospective wife or just the girl he slept with? For a few short weeks or for a lifetime?

'I think you'd like my home,' he said softly. 'You can hear the ocean as you're lying in bed, and when it's misty you can taste the salt of the sea. Come back with me.'

'I couldn't arrange it as quickly as that,' Kate said helplessly, fully aware that she was stalling for

time. It could be done and she knew it. The last
time she had left the cottage it had been at a few
hours' notice and she had not really cared what
had happened to it until some of the misery and
anger had worn off.

The reminder brought back more hurtful
memories, recollections that she had buried at the
back of her mind because the knowledge was still
bitter, but now brought to the surface by his
words.

Miles. Miles who had told her from the start of
their relationship that he had been married once
and never intended to be married again, and who
had been impressed by her open declaration that
she never wanted to be tied by a piece of paper
and a gold ring. Bold words. Words that she had
meant at the time, but had slowly come to regret
as time went on. She realised now that her
independence had attracted him, just as his air of
being a very self-sufficient man had drawn her, but
the characteristic had finally parted them because
she had changed her mind and he had not.

He had wanted her to live with him, had asked
her over and over again, and she had used the
excuse of her independence to avoid giving him an
answer. When she had finally told him the truth, it
had blown their affair sky-high and he had
accused her of dishonesty, accused her of trying to
trap him into marriage, accused her of other things
that even now she would not think about.

'You're too quiet,' Luke observed. 'Are you
thinking about it, or have you gone to sleep?' The
small joke came readily enough, but Kate sensed
his disquiet.

'I'm thinking,' she admitted, 'wondering if we
aren't going too quickly . . .'

'Quickly? My God, woman, I've been courting you for weeks!'

'Courting? That's a good old-fashioned word!'

'It's true,' he defended himself. 'I knew from the start that you were important to me. Remember that first evening when you played the piano with me? You touched my shoulder, and . . .'

'And what?'

'. . . I kind of went up in flames inside.'

Flames. Fire. Just how she had described her affair with Miles to Clare. Surely this wasn't going to be a carbon copy of that disaster?

'Really?' she asked.

'Yes, really,' Luke confirmed quietly. Then, 'Look at me.'

It was an effort to meet his eyes squarely when memories of Miles were beginning to haunt her, but she did so bravely and caught her breath at the expression that she saw in them. There was the fire. It was at the back of his eyes, making them seem darker and more alive than ever. His love was nakedly evident in his whole face, and she sighed when she saw it and went into his arms as if compelled by his magnetism, to be kissed with a loving passion that took her breath away.

He did mean it. It was all there in the mouth that fused with hers, the arms that held her against him, and the heart that hammered under her caressing hand. When she finally raised her head and looked at him she had to take a deep breath before she could find the words to give him.

'I do love you,' she said shakily, 'so very much,' and she pressed her lips to a pulse that beat jerkily at his throat.

'So why won't you say yes?'

It would be so easy. Yet she also wanted to have

the whole truth between them, and the truth was
that she wanted marriage. Her heart cried out for
that ring she had once told Miles she scorned, but
the mere recollection of that final ugly scene kept
her mouth firmly closed. Would he accuse her of
trying to pressure him? On the other hand, wasn't
it her right to know where she stood, to either be
assured of a future with him or told from the
beginning that it would be just a short-lived affair
until he found someone else to love?

She felt trapped. Never before had she admitted
to herself the basic reason for her split from Miles,
but Luke was inadvertently forcing her to face the
facts.

'We'll be travelling around,' he told her. 'Maybe
it'll give you some ideas for a new book. Part of
my next film will be shot in New Orleans. You'd
like it there.' He shook her gently and now his face
was concerned. 'I want you with me,' he said
simply.

It would be the easiest thing in the world to say
yes. To go back with him, to be with him for as
long as he wanted her, to try not to think about
the future. Yet she knew that she would, because
she recognised the sort of person that she was. Her
confidence was faked to some extent. Security,
something that she had never thought about a few
years ago, now seemed more important as she got
older. How could she explain that to Luke? Yet
she loved him, and the thought of being without
him finally decided her.

'Yes,' she said simply, 'I'll come . . .' and as his
face lit up with open joy, '. . . but you'll have to
give me a little time to sort everything out.' Would
he tell her to sell her cottage because she would
never be coming back?

'You won't regret it.' He lifted her hand and turned it over to place a kiss in her palm. 'I swear to you that you won't regret it.'

Now, at this moment, she had made him happy, so how could she be sorry about anything? And if the doubts returned, as she knew they would— well, then she would only have to think of this moment to remind herself of what she would be missing.

She drew his head down and kissed him, feeling him hold her tightly and not wanting to talk but just to have his physical closeness blot out all the uncertainties that she was trying to forget. Maybe, in the next four days, matters would clarify themselves. Maybe by the time he left for America she would be completely happy. They had four days.

CHAPTER NINE

FOUR days. Four days of being together, on their own, in the seclusion of the cottage and the quiet countryside around Toggleton. Four days when the sky had been as blue and bright as the light in Luke's eyes, and the sun had turned his fair hair into a halo of gold. Four days of rapturous solitude with the man she loved, basking in the bliss of knowing that she was loved just as deeply in return. Kate smiled involuntarily.

She stared through the side window of the big limousine and tried to recapture her favourite moments during those hours. There were so many to choose from, so many precious, intimate recollections that were etched for ever on her brain. How did she remember him best? Well, that was easy!

They had gone up to Chapel Hill and she had watched him as he stared out at the view. Then he had turned his head towards her, tilting it slightly, and his blue eyes had been alight with laughter, his blond hair tousled and blown back from his forehead by the breeze, and the long tanned column of his throat enhanced by his open necked shirt. Relaxed and off guard, it was a vivid picture of the Luke Arran she loved best. The man who liked animals, the man whose hands had the gentleness of a woman's as he cradled a kitten and yet the strength to unscrew the top of a ketchup bottle that she had thought could never be opened.

His hands had been gentle with her, too. She

remembered waking up one morning to find his forefinger tracing the line of her eyebrows, feathering across her cheek to her mouth with a touch so light and so delicate that it had been a mere whisper of a caress. The soft touch of his fingers and the lean hardness of his body close to hers in the big bed had, in a strange way, encapsulated Luke Arran for her. In him strength and gentleness were mixed in a combination that she found totally irresistible.

On one other morning, she recalled, she had woken up first and had propped herself up on to one elbow to watch him as he slept peacefully and quietly at her side. She had felt so protective towards him then, seeing him in the half-light of the dawn and realising that he looked younger with the lines smoothed from his face.

Contentedly she had waited for him to wake up, snugly aware of secrets shared and confidences exchanged in the darkness of the night and the intimacy of the bed in which they had slept. She had thought herself totally happy then, and had only realised how wrong she was when his eyes had opened and he had smiled at her. Then she had been happy.

Those four days had shown her just how much she needed him, and she believed that he needed her too. He had said that he did, and she had believed him, putting aside her doubts for their future in the belief that she could make him happy, and be happy herself with just a few short weeks if that was all the time they would have.

Stop it! She said the words sharply, roughly, to herself. It's over! Over and done with! Don't be such a fool!

Nine months and five days since she had last

seen him. A million hours. Half a lifetime. No, it couldn't be a million hours! She tried to work the sum out in her head, but her brain would not co-operate.

She had met him in the summer, when the days were bright, sparkling as their love, and she had existed through the worst of the winter, gritting her teeth at the ice outside her window and the never-ending ache of desolation gnawing away inside her. In a month or so it would be spring, but there was still no hope in her heart. She suspected that the warming rays of the sun would do nothing to cheer her, and the bleakness of the days she was living through matched the bleakness she felt inside. Nine months and five days!

'Niall, where are we going?' She turned her head to look at the man by her side in the back of the big car.

'I've told you. To a party,' he replied.

'Whose party? Why are you being so secretive?'

'I have my reasons.' Niall always had a reason, but this seemed so out of character that Kate was lost for a quick answer to his calmness. 'You look nice,' he added. 'I'm not sure I like the way you've grown your hair, but it looks good tonight.'

'You're my agent, not my father!'

'Of course, dear. Just making conversation.'

She would not admit it to him, but she too was pleased with the way the hairdresser had twisted it up into an immaculate pleat, softening the severity of the style with wings of hair that swept forward on to her cheeks.

As Niall did not seem inclined to talk, she returned her attention to the dark streets of London outside the window. It was raining, a depressing drizzle of wetness that had made her

reluctant to leave her hotel for the dubious
delights of a party she knew nothing about. Yet
Niall had insisted and she had not had the spirit to
oppose him.

She seemed to have very little energy for anything at the moment. It was not laziness, just an
inability to focus her attention on any project or
any activity. She was drifting and she knew it.

Clare knew it too. A Clare whom she had met
earlier that day for the first time since she had left
the cottage nine months before, and her friend had
been annoyed with her for disappearing without
leaving a forwarding address, and dismayed by her
callous disregard for Luke Arran's feelings. Kate
grimaced. Clare had not even liked Luke, but she
had still defended him. Kate remembered Clare's
blank astonishment when she had revealed that
she had been in Brixham for all the nine months,
but when she had added that she had been writing,
Clare had nodded.

Niall was pleased with what she had written.
Kate turned her head to look at the man by her
side, marvelling yet again at how this basically
ugly man, with his big nose, too-wide mouth and
aggressive jaw, could nevertheless be so attractive.

It was only recently that she had seen him in the
light of a friend. Before that he had been her
tormentor, her persecutor, the man who was trying
to make her write when she did not want to. She
had hated him for his insistence and been very
slightly afraid of his bullying tactics. Now, as he
looked at her and smiled, she wondered how she
could ever have misjudged him, for although she
had always trusted him, she had never before
thought of him as a friend.

She remembered that Niall had been at first

surprised and then delighted with what she had
written, but acting on his carefully worded
suggestion, she was using a second pen-name. She
saw, as he did, that the book was totally different
from anything she had produced before, but she
also knew that it was the best novel she had ever
written, and Niall, although generally wary of
committing himself, had agreed.

Now the manuscript was in his hands and she
really did not care what became of it. It had been
born out of her passionate feelings for Luke, and
when she had completed it, she had packed it off
to him and lapsed immediately into a period of
self-pity that she now despised herself for,
although, looking back, she was able to understand
what had caused it.

With the book completed she had lost her
catharsis, and had had no other way of giving an
outlet to her feelings. The book had been written
for her—Kate Fisher—and not for anyone else. In
the past she had studied her markets carefully,
setting out to entertain the people who would buy
her books and trying, with an honesty that was
part of her character, to give value for money.
This new book was different. She had written
exactly what she wanted to write, pouring out the
words in an agony of raw disillusionment, anger,
and anguished bewilderment.

She had not looked at it since, and for some
reason of its own her brain would not allow her
memory even to recall parts of it, but she knew
Niall had been startled by the change from her
normal output. It was powerful fiction, written
with a depth of intensity of which she had not
thought herself capable.

He had said it was different and of course it

was. She was different. Luke had taught her about love, shown her how close two people could be, and yet the final bond of trust, Kate knew now, had not been forged between them. Her fault, of course. She had held back out of a fear that her bubble of happiness would burst if she was careless of it. All her love for Luke was in that book, all her fears and worries poured out on paper because she had not been articulate enough to tell them to him. The writing was more mature, both in style and content, and she had reached into the depths of herself for the words to describe the love that was breaking her heart. Kate Fisher's personal statement.

Brixham. She sighed as she remembered her days in the small town she had fled to. There had been times when she would have sold her soul for a sight of his face again.

On clear evenings, when she had sat in the picture window of her rented fisherman's cottage high above the quay and looked over the harbour, she had yearned with every fibre of her being to have him beside her, sharing the scene with her. She had ached for him every time she had walked around the town, knowing how he would have loved the steep narrowness of the streets, and he was never out of her thoughts as she took her regular place on the harbour wall to watch the boats bobbing at anchor in the early evening.

The only time when she had been able to shut him out had been when she was working and when she was asleep, but the rest of the time he was always there, to the point where she sometimes thought she saw him on the street, and her heart would lurch painfully. The loneliness had been almost intolerable. It was only the novel she had

been working on that had kept her sane, and it
had been her companion and the outlet for all her
jumbled emotions. She sighed again.

'You sound tired,' said Niall, and she came back
to the present with a start.

'Just thinking,' she told him.

'What about? Brixham? Are you going to settle
down there?'

'I don't think so.' But she had no desire to
return to Toggleton either. Although it was her
home, and she still felt the tug of the place pulling
at her sometimes, how could she go back to the
cottage that she had shared with Luke? It had now
become a millstone. She could not bear to live
there again, but she could not bring herself to sell
it either, to have other people sleeping in the
bedroom that had been theirs for four days, to
have other people sunning themselves in the small
back garden as she and Luke had done.

'So what are you going to do?' Niall asked
insistently.

'I don't know.' She remembered that Clare had
asked exactly the same question, and had been
given the same answer. Suddenly the tears were
blinding her, and she turned her head away
hastily.

She had not thought she would ever be able to
cry again. Without meaning to, she turned her
thoughts back to those few days after Luke had
gone.

She had been packing to fly out to him. Her visa
was due to arrive any day and the cottage was to
be looked after by Clare and Miss Mole. She had
felt as if she was in some kind of limbo at the time,
torn between a frantic desire to see Luke again,
but afraid of the kind of life she was going to walk

into and her own ability to cope with it. Then she
had received the press cutting from an American
journal that showed Luke escorting a film actress,
not Sandy Gale, to a premiere. It had been
anonymous, of course, just like her letters, but the
message had, to her, seemed quite clear.

Clare had disagreed. Clare had urged her to
ask Luke what was going on, and had declared
that the other magazines and photographs that
arrived were all junk, maintaining that the actress
with whom Luke had been pictured holding hands
was probably just a friend. Kate had not listened.
She had told Luke, when he telephoned her, that
she was delaying her departure by a few days,
and when yet more photographs had arrived, she
had packed up and left Toggleton. Just like before.

There was a difference, she told herself
rebelliously. She had not been sent pictures of
Miles with someone else, and she had not loved
the dark-haired man as she had loved Luke Arran.
Still loved Luke Arran. That love was still as much
a part of her as it had been when she had spoken
to him for the last time, but she saw things more
clearly now. She realised that her honesty with
Miles, the cause of their relationship ending so
bitterly, had made her afraid of being truthful with
Luke and telling him all the things that she was
scared of. Things like fitting in with his way of life,
competing for him with other women more
beautiful than she was, and battling with her own
deeply-hidden insecurity.

There had been another reason too. She could
not bear to believe that the love they had shared
was not to last for ever. The thought of finally
being made as redundant as Nancy had been when
Luke had spent four days at her cottage frightened

her. She had rejected him before she could be
rejected by him.

Clare had told her, in their conversation that
morning, that Luke had been in touch with her
some months ago trying to find out where Kate
had gone. Clare had said that Luke was still in
love with her—or he had been those few months
ago—and her friend had urged her to try and
straighten out her life once and for all, imply-
ing with all Clare's usual bluntness that Kate
should go to America and find him again. Should
she?

'Where are we going?' She forced her thoughts
back to the present, afraid to dwell on the question
of her future.

'To a party.'

'I know that,' she told Niall impatiently. 'Whose
party?'

'You'll see.'

'Will you please stop being so mysterious and
tell me!'

He turned to grin at her. 'That's more like it!
That's more like the Kate I know. I wondered how
long it would take before I could needle you out of
your apathy.'

'Niall!'

His grin became broader. 'There's no mystery,'
he assured her. 'I just wanted to get you curious
and then angry. Anything's better than your
pathetic face ...'

'I am not pathetic!'

'No,' he agreed smoothly, 'not now.'

'The party, Niall, the party!'

'There's a film premiere tonight,' he told her.
'We could have gone to it, but in the mood you're
in at the moment, I didn't think you'd enjoy it. So

we're going to the party that's being held afterwards.'

'Oh.' This was not at all what she was expecting. She had guessed it was to be some kind of literary function. 'I didn't know you liked that kind of thing,' she commented.

'I don't—much. But the invitation came and I thought you might enjoy going. It could be interesting.'

'Who'll be there? The people who are in the film?'

'Yes.'

'Well,' she asked impatiently, 'who *is* in the film?'

'No one terribly important. Luke Arran, Sandy Gale . . .'

Suddenly the car was too small. It was suffocating her, closing in on her, and as she took a deep, shuddering breath, she felt perspiration bead her top lip and her forehead. Suddenly she felt cold and faint.

'I don't want to go,' she said weakly. 'Niall . . .'

'Too late!' He was looking out of the side window of the car away from her, and apparently her voice did not alert him to the possibility of there being anything amiss.

'Niall, please!' She laid a hand on his arm and he turned to her.

'Something wrong?'

'Yes . . . no . . .' How much did he know? Did he know anything at all? Was there something planned in all this, or was it some terrible coincidence?

'Make up your mind!' he grinned.

'Do you know Luke Arran?'

'Slightly.'

'How?'

His face was full of surprise, but for the life of her she could not tell if the innocent look was feigned or genuine.

'My dear Kate, I do have other authors on my lists as well as you. I have dealings with all sorts of people.'

'Sorry.' She had been gently snubbed and she knew it. In recent months he had been very good to her and perhaps she had taken up more of his time than she should. She was grateful to him, but was she grateful enough to sit and watch Luke at a party with Sandy Gale and the other actors? Could she do it without weeping or showing any hint of the turmoil of emotions that now raged inside her? The faintness was receding, but she still felt cold and shaky, and Niall was watching her more closely.

'Do you feel all right?' he asked her.

'What? Oh, yes.' She was preoccupied with questions that she could not ask, answers that she dared not think about, and the sudden giddiness of hope that she could not quench. To see him again—tonight! She would have preferred it to have been a less public occasion, but then again her common sense asserted itself. He would be too busy to take much notice of his guests. He would be meeting important people, guided by the ubiquitous Ray, and it would be an occasion similar to the party at Pike House. The initiative could still be hers if she wanted it to be.

Initiative? What initiative? She was going to be seeing a man from whom she had run away several months ago. A man whom she had treated badly and who would have every right to ignore her.

'Do you know Luke Arran?' Niall asked her

suddenly. She looked at him and nodded. 'Did you
meet him when he was making the film?'

'Yes.'

Something in her tone must have worried him.
He turned in his seat and took her hand.

'Look,' he began awkwardly, 'if you really don't
want to go, then we can still back out. If there's
something going on that I don't know about . . .'
and then, with a hint of exasperation, '. . . oh hell,
Kate! I don't know what you're thinking! We
don't have to go . . .'

Yes, but if they didn't, she might never find the
courage to seek him out again. Just to see him; to
be in the same room and perhaps hear him laugh.
She had loved to hear him laugh, just as she had
loved the blue of his eyes and the curve of his
mouth.

'What do you want to do?' Niall interrupted her
thoughts yet again.

'We'll go,' she said decisively. 'I'm sorry, Niall, I
didn't mean to be awkward.'

'You're always awkward,' he told her cheerfully,
'but you're also talented and beautiful, so I
suppose I shall have to put up with you.'

Luke had called her beautiful—so many times.
Everything that she saw and everything that was
said now seemed to remind her of him. Would it
ever stop?

Heart-wrenchingly she was taken back to the
time when they had spent a day on the sands of a
small, little-known beach where they had soaked
up the sun for hours, just talking and laughing and
kissing. Such a happy day. She could remember, as
if it was yesterday, the lean, athletic figure of the
man who had waded out of the sea after his swim
with the sunlight glinting off the droplets of water

on his shoulders and his hair plastered back
against his skull making his face look even thinner
than usual. He had reminded her of some sea-god
rising from the depths of the ocean, and she had
sat on her towel and stared at him, only coming
out of her entranced state when the seaweed that
he had trailed up the beach with him was wound
around her shoulders. Then he had called her
beautiful.

Her heart was thumping sickly now, and unobtrusively she tried to breathe deeply and slowly to
calm herself. She was torn two ways, between a
desire to see him, to try and explain what had
happened all those months ago, and a feeling that
she wanted to run away and hide. Again.

No, she decided firmly. She had run away twice
before. She would not do so again.

It was obvious that no expense had been spared in
the decoration of the big restaurant where Luke's
party was to be held. It was bright with flowers
and lanterns and streamers, reminding Kate of a
carnival. She sat in her chair, nervously drinking
champagne, and she had just begun to regain her
confidence amid the easy friendliness of the other
people on their table when a stir of activity
announced the arrival of the celebrities.

'There he is,' Niall murmured in her ear.

She did not need to be told. She had eyes only
for the man who was crossing the open area of the
dance floor, nodding to the people who began to
applaud him. Holding his arm possessively, Sandy
Gale looked dramatic and very beautiful in a
sapphire blue dress with a low-cut neckline and
diamonds encircling her throat and wrist, but Kate
only spared her a passing glance.

She had never seen Luke in anything other than jeans and a denim jacket or casual trousers and a sports coat, and in evening dress he looked taller and broader than she remembered. He was smiling, he seemed relaxed and confident, and her heart lurched sharply as she resisted the temptation to push past Niall and go to him.

'They make a good-looking couple,' the girl on her left said softly. 'I wonder if he bought her the jewellery.'

'I wonder,' Kate echoed, but she only watched Luke, her body tense with jealousy as she saw him smile at something Sandy said and take her arm to lead her to their table, which was out of Kate's line of vision. Unconsciously she twisted the silver bracelet on her arm; the token of Luke's love.

Now that Luke had arrived she could not concentrate on any topic of conversation for long, although she did listen to one man's assessment of the film, and was pleased by the general opinion that it would be a success. Luke deserved it. It also gave her an excuse to approach him, but she shrank from the idea of walking up to his table under the eyes of all the other guests. She just did not have that kind of confidence. On the other hand, she did not want him to see her for the first time when she danced past him with another man, and she racked her brain for inspiration.

The minutes passed and she hovered agonisingly over a decision, but as she glanced around the room in an effort to appear casual, she saw Tony quite close to her table, and as she stared at him their eyes met. She saw him recognise her, saw the frown that crossed his face, saw him hesitate, and then abruptly return the way he had come. Would he tell Luke?

Another five minutes dragged by, and with every second her tension increased. Where was he? Had Tony told him that she was here? Did he intend to ignore her? She would not blame him if he did.

Niall's eyes suddenly went beyond her and she sensed someone standing behind her chair. The other two couples stopped talking and smiled, but Kate did not dare to turn her head.

'Good evening.' His voice was very formal and very precise.

'Hello, Luke.' She turned in her seat and looked up at him. 'How are you?'

'Fine, thanks.' His voice was as casual as hers had been. 'Are you enjoying yourself?'

'Yes, thank you.'

What else could she say? They had observed the formalities and now she was lost for words. There was a moment's silence while she looked at him dumbly and he seemed to hesitate, and then he was asking her to dance.

He allowed her to precede him to the edge of the floor, and as she turned to wait for him he slipped an arm around her waist and manoeuvred her expertly into the crowd of dancers. She would not have expected that a man who was almost addicted to well cut but faded jeans and casual shirts would display a talent for ballroom dancing, but Luke did. He appeared to be the exception to every rule she had ever known.

'Where the hell have you been?' His voice was no more than a whisper of sound, but the vehemence in it was a shock and she leaned back a little against his arm to see his face.

'Devon,' she said simply.

'Devon?' he echoed blankly. 'Why there?'

'I used to go there on holiday when I was a child . . .'

'. . . and you don't seem to have grown up much since.'

'If you're going to be insulting, then I'm going to leave!'

'Really?' His arm around her waist had all the implacability of a steel hawser and the fingers that gripped hers so tightly that they hurt were a warning to her not to pull away.

The brief clash of words depressed her. If all they could do was to exchange barbed comments then she was lost before she started. How could she explain her feelings and apologise adequately for her mistakes to this stone-faced stranger?

'Luke . . .' she began tentatively.

'What?'

'I'm sorry.'

'For what?'

'For . . .' She was not sure how to phrase her words, '. . . for coming back into your life like this. It wasn't my idea. Niall brought me and wouldn't let me say no.'

'I know him,' he admitted, 'but it never occurred to me that he'd bring you.'

'I'm sorry,' she said again, aware of how inadequate the words sounded.

'Yes, so am I.' She felt him take a deep breath that came out sounding like a sigh of regret. 'You know, I was happy tonight . . .'

'I hear the film is good. Congratulations.'

'To hell with the film!' It had been the wrong thing to say and Kate winced from the harsh voice. 'I was hoping you were going to say you were sorry for walking out on me. We had four beautiful days. Didn't they mean anything?'

'Of course they did!' It was ridiculous to be discussing this in the middle of a dance floor. She had a desire to reach up and smooth the deep lines from his forehead and comfort him, but his expression was remote and she did not dare.

'Oh yes? Not enough, apparently.'

Nothing in her life had meant more, but how could she tell him that now? People were watching them covertly and how could she talk about love under their scrutiny? Why had he chosen this place, of all places, to talk to her again? It was too public.

'Did they mean that much to you?' she countered quietly. 'Some kind person kept sending me articles about you ... pictures of you with someone else. It didn't take you long, Luke.'

'For ...' He bit off the words he was going to say, but she did not dare to look up into his face. She kept her gaze on the dancers around them over his shoulder, and only the sudden tension in his body told her how angry he was. 'It was publicity,' he said at last, 'that's all. Why in hell didn't you ask me? I'd've told you.' Deliberately he steered her towards a corner of the dance floor and then his words of outrage poured into her ears. 'Did I believe one word in those letters you got? Did I? Did I ... for one moment ... doubt you?'

'You accused me of writing that article.'

He cursed then, bitterly and briefly, and she flinched.

'Okay,' he said at last, 'I accept that. But I came to apologise to you, didn't I? Why couldn't you have trusted me?'

The question was asked with a soft weariness that brought the tears to Kate's eyes.

'It was all right when I was with you,' she offered lamely. 'Only after you'd gone, all the doubts were there . . .'

'What doubts? You never talked to me about doubts. I thought you were happy.'

'I was!' She had to defend those four days. She would not deny their importance. They had been the best four days of her life.

'I was happy too.' Suddenly Luke's voice altered. 'I was so much in love with you. I went home and I started looking at houses because I thought you might not like mine. I bought a desk and an electric typewriter so that you could work when you wanted to, and I told all my friends that the most fantastic girl in the world was coming out to the States to be with me. I told my parents too.' Kate closed her eyes in appalled horror. 'And then you weren't there when I called you . . .' the quiet voice seemed lost in a fog of memories, '. . . and your letters stopped coming . . . and I was so scared! I called Clare and she told me you'd gone, and I couldn't believe it. I waited for you . . .' a sudden, mirthless parody of a chuckle. 'I trusted you to come to me when you could. I knew you were independent and I knew you were used to living by yourself. I just thought you needed a little time. Clare told me you liked to do things in your own way. Then I woke up one morning and realised that I'd lost you . . . and I was lost too. I needed you, you see, and you weren't there.'

Kate willed herself not to cry. She had been so wrong, so stupidly, arrogantly, selfishly, wilfully wrong. She had misjudged the depth of his love, and had been too frightened of it to be honest with him.

How could she explain it all so that he would

understand? Would she ever be able to make him
believe that she had suffered too? Would it be
possible for him to understand that she had only
acted out of a belief that she was not strong
enough to accept the consequences of their love?

'Don't you have anything to say?' His voice
mocked her now and he had obviously recovered
his poise as he turned her and steered her back
into the throng of dancers in a move that she was
sure was calculated to inhibit her answer. As it did.
'Aren't you going to try to justify what you did?'

'I did what I thought was right.' As soon as the
words were out she regretted them. She should not
be defending herself because there was no defence.
He was quite right—she had not trusted him.

'*You* did what *you* thought was right?' He
stressed the two words deliberately. 'My God, that
says it all, doesn't it? It was our future you decided
all by yourself. You didn't give any thought to
how I might feel. You didn't tell me about these
doubts you're now saying you had. Why? Didn't I
have a right to know?'

'I was scared of spoiling things.'

Her answer to that was a sudden and ominous
silence, but she still did not dare to look at him,
enduring the tension that was building between
them while it stretched her nerves almost to
breaking point.

The music stopped. People applauded. Suddenly
Kate was free of his restraining arms and she
turned away automatically before strong, slim
fingers clamped themselves around her wrist.

'Smile!' Luke spoke the word between his teeth.
'People are looking at us. Smile, damn you!'

It was the least she could do for him. She forced
her stiff lips to curve upwards into a travesty of a

grin, but he would not release her wrist so that she could clap with the others. She was forced to stand at his side and know that she was being watched and endure the way his fingers dug into her skin. He had done that once before, she remembered, only the last time he had kissed the marks in unhappy acknowledgement of his temper.

It was hot on the dance floor. Kate could feel beads of perspiration freckling her nose and her forehead. It occurred to her that she might be going to faint and she was glad of the pain in her wrist. It was something that she could cling on to, something to focus her attention on. When the music began again, Luke took her back in his arms.

'Can we talk about this somewhere else?' she asked at last. 'This isn't the time or the place.'

'Is there anything left to talk about?' he countered quickly.

'All that you've said is true.' Suddenly she felt her confidence return. 'But it's more complicated than you're making it sound . . .'

'Is it? Doesn't it all come down to a simple question of trust?' He was holding her so tightly that she could not lean back and see his face, but the long line of his body was pressed closely against her own in the slow rhythm of the waltz, and suddenly she felt weak with love for him. 'You didn't trust me enough to talk to me.' His voice drove onwards implacably. 'You didn't love me enough to let me help you. You didn't want to give up your independence because it scared you to know you were relying on someone else. You've been alone too long, Kate. You're selfish.'

Clare had said the same thing. Was it true? Maybe she did not have the courage to give at least part of the responsibility for her own life into someone else's hands.

'Please ...' she was begging him now and she did not care, '... can't we find some other place to talk?' His body was seducing hers without even trying and all the love inside her was screaming to him to listen.

'Sure.' She felt him shrug. 'I'll give you the name of my hotel and you can join me there later if you like. Maybe we can salvage something of the evening.'

She did not wonder why he had suddenly capitulated so easily, she was just grateful for his agreement.

'Thank you,' she said softly. 'I just want a chance to explain things to you.'

'Explain?' Luke's arms loosened and she looked up into his face and saw one eyebrow arch upwards in surprise. 'Oh, I don't think we'll get time to talk, honey,' and the smile that flickered around his mouth told her the rest of the story. Her eyes widened in shocked disbelief and then she stared steadily into the thin, handsome face for a last long moment before she turned on her heel and walked away from him.

She did not see Nancy until she was almost at the edge of the dance floor, but her feet did not falter. She did not care what Nancy said to her. Nothing was important any more. Luke had shown only too clearly what he thought of her and she knew that nothing that Nancy could say could hurt her.

Face to face they stared at one another, then Nancy smiled.

'I told you that Luke was mine,' she said softly.

'You did, didn't you?' Kate admitted. A couple

on their way to the dance floor pushed past them, and in allowing them to get by her, Kate turned slightly so that Nancy was looking away from it as she talked to her. 'You sent me those pictures, didn't you.' Kate did not make the words an accusation, just a statement of fact.

'Yes.'

'And the letters.'

'Yes. You can't prove a thing.'

No, she couldn't, but Luke had seen them talking and was walking towards them.

'No, I can't,' Kate agreed readily. 'One person's word against another's.' She was trying very hard to focus Nancy's attention entirely on her, and she did not dare to look beyond her to where Luke was rapidly closing the gap between them.

'I suppose you wrecked my house as well,' she said, and then wondered if she had pushed too far. This was a far more serious incident and she was not sure that Nancy would admit to it. 'No,' she corrected herself quickly, 'perhaps it wasn't you. That demands a lot more courage than just sending letters through the post. You wouldn't have had the nerve!'

'Oh yes, I would!' Vanity had got to the girl where everything else might have failed. And Luke was close now.

'It was really you?' Kate did not know from where she was finding the self-discipline or the courage to continue the conversation. One small part of her, the part that had not been numbed by her encounter with Luke, was hysterically commanding her to lash out at this girl for what she had done, to assault her physically and verbally, to punish her. 'I don't believe it!'

'Of course it was me!' Nancy's voice was low,

but Luke was directly behind her. 'It wouldn't be the first time I've had to warn someone off him. I told you that he was mine, but you couldn't take the hint, could you? The letters would have been enough for most people, but not for you. I enjoyed breaking up your house, and I'd do it again if I had to.'

Now, for the first time, Kate allowed herself to look directly into Luke's eyes and to read the dismay and the anger there.

'You heard that?' she asked coldly. 'See what some people will do in the name of love? And you wonder why I'm scared of it?'

'Kate ...' She saw quite clearly that he was appalled by what he had heard and Nancy's face, as she turned to look at her employer, was the colour of bleached bones. '... What do you want to do about her?' Luke asked quietly.

'Nothing.' She hated Nancy, hated the kind of love that the other girl had for Luke, and could not bear the expression on his face. 'I just want to be left alone. Just leave me alone!'

CHAPTER TEN

By the time the big car had delivered her back to her hotel, the headache that Kate had used as an excuse to Niall had become a reality and she felt as though a band was tightening around her forehead every time she moved.

Niall was anxious and solicitous, but she could not bear to be fussed and refused his offers of help, insisting that he go back to the party and thankfully closing the door of her room behind her.

Kicking off her shoes, she dragged the pins from her hair until it fell around her shoulders, then she pulled back the covers of the bed and climbed in, still fully dressed. Turning on her side to curl up into a ball of misery, she pulled the covers over her head, and then she began to cry.

The night was endless. The two aspirins that she took had no effect on her blinding headache, and when she took two more after only an hour, barely aware of the risk, they only managed to reduce the pain to a dull ache. Her eyes were gritty and swollen from crying, and despite turning the heating up in the room, she still felt sick and shivery.

At six in the morning she stripped off her dress, washed her face, changed and ordered coffee to be brought to her room. From six until nine she alternately paced the room, reminding herself of a caged animal, and lay on her bed staring at the ceiling as she let the tears well up again.

A tap on her door at nine o'clock heralded the
arrival of a single red rose. At first she thought it
was from Niall, but when she read Luke's name on
the small white card, she opened the box, took out
the flower and ripped it into shreds, sitting on the
floor five minutes later to cry over the torn pieces
and to wonder why he had sent it.

She had an appointment with Niall at ten, but
she left herself no time for a proper breakfast and
had to take a taxi to get to his office on time. Her
head felt full of cotton wool, but she felt that all
her tears had been shed and she met him with
composure.

'You look like death,' was his greeting.

'Thanks very much,' she said wearily, and seated
herself in one of the armchairs in his office,
crossed her legs and lit a cigarette.

'Do you have any coffee?' she asked hopefully.

'Of course. Would you like a sandwich too?'

'That sounds lovely.' She made an effort to pull
herself together and smiled wanly at him. 'I'm
sorry,' she apologised, 'I had to rush to get here.'

'You don't have to apologise to me.' Niall
picked up the telephone and spoke to his secretary,
then seated himself at his desk and looked at her.
'Are you well enough to talk?' he asked, and his
concern was obvious.

'Yes, thanks.' She had no time for pleasantries.
'What do you want to see me for?'

'It's about your book.' She noticed that he had
the manuscript in front of him. 'There's just one or
two small details . . .'

'I don't want to do any more work on it,' she
broke in. 'I just want to forget about it.'

'Do you really mean that?'

'Indeed I do!'

'Kate . . .' he hesitated, then said levelly, 'do you realise how big a success this book could have? It's a beautiful piece of writing and it's commercial, and quite honestly far better than anything you've ever written before. You could make your name with this.'

'Really?'

'You don't care, do you?' He came around from his chair to perch on the edge of his desk, and she eyed him warily as he looked at her.

'A year ago I'd have given an arm and a leg to hear you say that.'

'And today?'

'Today?' She shrugged. 'I've got a lot on my mind. Writing used to be the most important thing in my life, but at the moment . . .' At the moment all that there was in her life was one big ache of regret because of a man called Luke Arran.

'Would it cheer you up if I told you I'd practically sold the film rights? All it needs is some signatures.'

'What?' Shaken out of her apathy, she stared at him.

'Good news, isn't it?'

'I don't know. The book isn't even out yet! Who are you negotiating with?'

'Luke Arran.'

'Oh no!' Stunned, Kate stared at him incredulously. 'No!' she said again, 'not him! Anyone but him.'

'You should be pleased.' The satisfied, faintly smug expression on Niall's face was fading.

'I don't want to see it turned into a film. How can they do it? It isn't suitable . . .'

'Luke Arran thinks it is.'

'He can't have it. I won't let him have it.'

Angrily she stubbed her cigarette out and rose to her feet. 'I won't agree to it, Niall,' she said flatly. 'I can't . . . won't . . .' A new thought struck her. 'How did he know? Who told him?' And then, 'How well do you really know him?'

'Sit down and we'll talk about it.'

'I don't want to sit down!' Angrily she fumbled in her bag for another cigarette, but her hands trembled as she tried to light it.

'I thought you'd given them up,' observed Niall.

'I have—practically. I only smoke a few a day.'

'Still too many. Now sit down, Kate, and listen to me.'

She knew that tone of voice. This was Niall at his most assertive, and she realised that he intended to have his say. Meekly she sat on the edge of her chair, refusing to meet his eyes, and said quietly:

'It's my book, Niall. My baby. Luke Arran isn't going to get his hands on it.'

'Why not? It's tailor-made for him.'

'I know.'

She met his eyes and he nodded, as if she had just confirmed some truth that he had only guessed at, but before he could speak, the sandwiches and coffee were brought in, and when Kate made no move to pour it out he busied himself with the cups.

Kate was confused and worried. Luke seemed to be deliberately trying to create a link between them, but why? What was he expecting her to do? Had he guessed, as Niall had obviously guessed, that the main character in her book had been based on him? It had been a dangerous thing to do, but at the time she had not cared. Now she was afraid. Could he sue her? Could he prove that the Michael Haynes of the book and Luke Arran were the same person?

He would play the part so well. He would be perfect. Was he playing some kind of game with her? After the bitterness of last night's scene would he withdraw his offer anyway?

'Tell me how it happened,' she said quietly.

Niall returned to his large teak desk and steepled his fingers together while he considered her for a moment.

'It's very simple,' he said carefully. 'Luke Arran owns a production company in the States. The initial approach came from one of his executives who was specifically interested in your work. Mention was made of a screenplay that maybe you could write, but the whole thing was rather vague. I was surprised at the contact because . . .' he shrugged and smiled, '. . . well, there are better writers in the world, my dear. Anyhow, I'd just had your manuscript, so I showed it to this man and he liked it. Luke Arran flew in a week ago and read it for himself. When he'd finished he said he wanted the film rights and we discussed the matter. He'll pay dearly for them, but he doesn't seem to care. He just seems determined to turn that book of yours into a film, come hell or high water. Of course,' Niall nodded, 'I didn't know until yesterday that you two knew one another. No one bothered to tell me that.'

'If he has the rights then no one else can make the film, can they? Perhaps that's the idea,' said Kate, almost to herself.

'I doubt it. Not from the way he was talking.'

'Hmm.' She bit into a sandwich. 'I'll have to think about this, Niall.'

'You won't get a better deal ... if you get another deal at all.'

'I honestly don't know that I want to see this particular book turned into a film at all.' She sipped her coffee and looked at him, almost smiling at the expression of amazement on his face.

'Now look here ...' Niall had a temper and it was coming slowly to the boil.

'Let me think about it,' Kate pleaded. 'Just for a day or so.'

She would go and see him and persuade him to drop the matter. Was that what he was expecting her to do? Why hadn't he mentioned the subject last night?

'Look ...' Niall was trying to be placatory, 'I don't know what your relationship with this man is ... and I don't need to be told. I took you along to that party last night because I got an invitation. I wasn't asked to bring you and I only did it because I thought you might like to see the man before I told you the news.'

She was not sure how to react to that piece of news. The sight of her last night must really have knocked Luke off balance.

'I see,' she said thoughtfully, a little lost for words.

'You're going to see him?'

'Yes.'

'Well, he's left his hotel, but I know where he's gone. If it's really important ...'

'It is.' She met his stare equably.

'Okay.'

At six o'clock that evening Kate arrived at the wide, imposing wrought iron gates of a big house in Suffolk, and through them she could see the dark bulk of a gatehouse twenty feet away. The gatehouse where Luke was staying for a few days.

It had been a long, slow, cold train ride, and the subsequent trip by taxi had been little better. She paid it off, hoping never to see it again, and pulled up the collar of her coat against the cold wind as it moved away into the darkness. Although it was still early evening it was very black, and there were no lights visible at the small stone house, and no street lights to help her find her way. She wished she had brought a torch. She wished she had curbed her impetuosity in coming so far without a thought of how she was going to get back. She wished for Luke's understanding when she met him.

With the thought that she would get nowhere by standing around, she pushed tentatively at one of the big gates, and was both relieved and surprised when it swung open without the smallest squeak. She waited for dogs to bark, for someone to demand what she was doing there, but as the silence lengthened she stepped through the gate, closed it carefully behind her and then walked briskly in the direction of the dark, unwelcoming house, slightly unnerved by the quietness of her surroundings.

The gatehouse door, old and sturdy, had no knocker and she could find no bell. She rapped on the wood with her knuckles, and when no one answered, she tapped harder. Still no one came.

Frustrated, uncertain, she looked around and saw the gravel path that skirted the house, flanked on the other side by thick bushes. It looked uninviting and somehow sinister, but Kate did not see what else she could do. She had come so far and faced so much that she could not endure the idea of going tamely away without finding out for certain whether anyone was at home or not. The prospect of walking down the lonely road to a telephone box to call for another taxi was even more daunting than the darkness of the path.

As she rounded the corner of the house, she could see a sliver of light coming through a gap in the curtains that covered narrow french windows, and after a moment's hesitation, praying that she would not be caught, she tiptoed to the window and peered in.

Somehow it was an anticlimax. She had half expected to find Luke with another woman so that she could go away and justify all her doubts and opinions of him in a glow of self-righteous anger, but he was alone.

He sat comfortably in an armchair, his legs crossed, and an open book on his lap. A big log fire warmed him and a curl of cigar smoke rose from an ashtray on a small table at his elbow. Handel's Water Music underlined the peacefulness of the scene, and Kate resented his air of serenity that contrasted strongly with her own turbulent emotions.

She stayed where she was for another few minutes, savouring the sight of his profile etched against the panelling of the room and the light from the fire and table lamps that highlighted the shining blond hair that was just a little longer than she remembered it to be.

Rapping lightly on the glass at last, she saw his head come up alertly. She knocked again and he came to the french windows and drew back the curtains to stare at her incredulously. The glass was between them and now she was impatient to talk to him and becoming colder by the minute as a chill wind made her shiver.

'Please open the door!' she called. 'It's freezing out here!'

For a moment she thought he was going to refuse. His hand hovered over the catch while his eyes searched her face as if looking for some clue to her presence, but when she blew on her hands and met his stare imploringly, he unlocked the door, letting the warmth of the room embrace her and draw her inside. She turned to watch him close the doors again and then she smiled.

'Hello.' Her voice was unintentionally husky. 'How are you?'

'Fine.' His response was mechanical.

'Can I talk to you for a minute?' Kate pulled off the fur hat that she had been wearing and threw it on to a nearby chesterfield, aware with each second that passed that his surprise at seeing her was an advantage that she would soon lose.

'We have something to discuss?' He had recovered more quickly than she had expected, and she hated the cold, clipped tone of his voice.

'Nancy,' she said quietly and quickly. 'What about Nancy?' It was the first thing that came into her head.

'She went back to the States this morning. Why? Have you changed your mind about her? You want to call in the police? I think it's too late for that.'

'I just wanted to know what had happened, that's all.'

'She's gone.' It was a flat statement made without any hint of emotion. 'I'm sorry it had to be one of my staff who hurt you so much.' The tone of voice denied the apology.

'It wasn't your fault.'

They stood facing one another, and Kate met his gaze and wondered frantically what had happened to the Luke she loved. In Toggleton he had been a relaxed, laughing, happy man. At the party he had been passionately angry and the emotion had given him a vitality that she had found exciting. Now there seemed to be nothing. His face was a bland mask and it was like looking at a stranger. Was he really so indifferent?

'Was that all you wanted?' The polite question suggested that she was wasting his time.

'No.' One of his eyebrows quirked upwards in a way that she had at one time found irresistibly endearing but now she found supercilious. 'Oh, Luke, don't be like this!' Her exasperation loosened her tongue. 'I've come to talk to you . . . to try to explain everything . . .'

'So explain.' He leaned back against the wall behind him and folded his arms, but his expression remained remote and unreadable.

'Not like this!' She would not be the prisoner at the bar. She would not allow him to sit in judgement over her.

'Then like what?' He levered himself away from the wall to stand erect. 'What do you want, exactly? There's no one here but us. Isn't this private enough for you?'

'I can't tell you anything when you look at me like that!' Goaded, she snapped the answer back at him.

'Can't change my face. Should I turn my back to you? Would that make it easier?'

'You're impossible!' She would never have imagined that he could defeat her so easily. She could not see even a glimpse of the compassion that she had thought was an integral part of the man she loved.

'Honey, if I'm impossible ... what does that make you?' His American drawl became more pronounced. 'You started all this. You left me ... remember?'

'I can't explain while you look so ... so grim!'

'You want me to smile?' The even white teeth appeared briefly as he parted his lips. 'Will this do?'

'All right.' It was not going to work. He had armoured his heart against her and she could not breach his defences. If he had loved her, then he could do so no longer. The Luke Arran she loved so much seemed to have disappeared somewhere deep inside him and this arrogant stranger bore little relation to him. 'You win,' she continued quietly. 'Again. I'm not going to fight you ...' Stupid word! Of course she didn't want to fight him! She wanted to yield to his superior strength—both physical and mental—and quietly and unobtrusively give up her independence for the greater joy of his protection. He was not going to allow it. He was going to give her nothing, not one word of encouragement or one sign that there was anything left between them. He was going to show her nothing but mild, sardonic amusement and that, above everything else, she could not bear. She just had one last string to her bow. One last way to keep a single link between them so that he could not go out of her life for ever.

'I want to talk to you about my book.' She took a deep breath as his face changed to become even more wary.

'You mean my film rights.'

'No one's going to make a film out of that

book,' she said quietly. 'It's special and it isn't suitable.'

'I say that it is.'

'I'm sorry.' She shook her head. 'Neither you nor Niall nor anyone else can make me change my mind. It's my book and no-one's going to influence me.' He was a determined man. He would fight her for those rights.

'Has anyone ever made you do anything you don't want to do?' His eyes challenged her, and the words that she wanted to say stuck in her throat.

Yes, she wanted to say, you. You made me fall in love with you. You wouldn't leave me alone when I asked you to. You wouldn't let me sleep in a chair when I wanted to. You made me show you that letter. You taught me what it was like to share everything with another human being. You made me love you, damn you!

'Never mind.' The journey, her tussle with Niall, lack of sleep, had suddenly made her unutterably weary. 'I don't think you'd understand if I told you.'

Where she would go she did not know, but she had to escape from the warmth of this cosy room with the cheerful glow of its log fire. Because she was cold. Chilled through to her bones by one man's rejection of her.

'Do you mind if I leave by the front door?' She was crossing the room as she spoke. 'I might be able to see where I'm going better.'

She walked swiftly across the small panelled hall, knowing that at any other time she would have stopped to admire the grained patterns of the wood, but now being solely concerned with putting some distance between the two of them. She tugged open the heavy front door to admit a